Also by Richard Oh

Heart of the Night

Ferry Tan

RICHARD OH

the Pathfinders of LOVE

Richard Oh took a degree in English Literature and Creative Writing at University of Wisconsin, Madison, USA. He lives in Jakarta with his wife and three children.

GAMELAN PRESS

GAMELAN PRESS

Published by Gamelan Press,
Cempaka Putih Timur No.14, Jakarta 10510, Indonesia
richoh@qbworld.com

Book design by Dedi Sugianto
Photograph by Fery R. Tan

ISBN 979-95692-0-6

Printed in Singapore

3 5 7 9 10 8 6 4 2

for all
who suffer
in silence

1

*O*n a day like this, with the fading light dappling the leaves, a slight breeze wafting in through the harbor and the cityscape unfolding in its tranquil span, nothing could have completed a simple man's pleasure than breathing it all in. The pungent, the sultry, the sweet, the vague passing fragrances, anything, even the putrid, the bland or acrid smell of the city would do to start the day. But none penetrated through Jailudin's blocked olfactory membranes. For years, he witnessed the passing light dribble across the leaves, dance on the water on the ponds, toying, teasing, and cajoling on the children's faces. Not a whiff from nature's treasure trove of scents could link itself to Jailudin's sense of smell. The maelstrom of scents, imbued, absorbed in abundance and naturally available for most people, remained doggedly unattainable, distant and obdurately elusive like an opaque wall that refused to be struck down.

For the life of him, he couldn't remember when it started to plague him. He wondered once whether it was one of those ailments, not unlike incontinence or Parkinson's disease, that afflicted one when one approached senility. Yet a brief general check up brought a clean bill of health and a smirk on the nurse's face. She knowingly acknowledged that for sure there might be something astray with regards to Jailudin's olfactory system; they were underutilized! With that the entire staff in Dr. Kemal's office broke into uncontrollable guffaw.

Relying more on the acuity of his sight rather than his snout for his profession, Jailudin comforted himself that the imperfection in his nose had notably sharpened his sense of imagery. It seemed that the 'defect' had considerably enhanced his instinctive feel for the right photographic image to go with each news item. And it was by no sheer coincidence that his photographs had been sought after by news organizations around the region. The images of chaos on the streets of Jakarta, splashed across the globe during May riots, had for the most part been purchased from his office, JPhotography.

Such achievements in the face of harsh economic reality had brought a sense of comfort and tremendous security to Jailudin's simple world. Such random, intractable reflections had never prefigured in his daily frantic pace, until this morning.

He scratched his head in absolute bafflement. It was a quaint aberration of behavior. The precarious feeling of having been to the brink of danger and back in one piece must have had something to do with it. He took ten solid rolls of film on the harrowing Ketapang Incident, the inner-city conflict between the Muslims and the Catholics. The Muslims, acting in rash fury on hearsay of Catholics burning down their mosque, went berserk, killing a dozen people and bringing down in flames by last count eleven churches. Jailudin had prided himself to be first at the scene with Sheryl and captured the havoc when it was still reasonably safe to do so. The sheer madness went beyond logical explanation. Without rhyme and reason, at the signal of a maddening clarion call for battle from a single human being, the entire area turned into a battle zone. The blood-thirsting mob rampaged, burnt and killed anyone that stood in the way, leaving behind charred bodies, torched vehicles and smashed windows. Jailudin had clicked away, nonchalantly, a professional at work behind filtered lenses.

It must have been the adrenaline pump left over from the assignment. Or could it be because it was his birthday today? Hitting the big four, not a particularly auspicious number in any culture, and the fact that not a single breathing, kicking, living soul knew about it, that must have been the irascible feeling behind all these wild ruminations. What on earth drove him so hard? Living by himself, with no particular expensive hobby, no one special woman to buy presents for, nor ownership of precious objects that required an expensive maintenance, he had every reason to sit back and take it easy. He had worked enough long hours and earned enough money to deserve some peace and quiet.

Buzz. The vibrating buzz from his cellular phone, tied inevitably nowadays with the breaking of his day, emanated from his knapsack.

"Hi J," it was Sheryl, the American freelance journalist. For over a month now she and Jailudin had formed a sort of writer-photographer pact. Jailudin helped her get the leads for her stories and on her side she helped him sell some of his photographs. "What's clicking today, my friend?"

"Same tedious stuff, except this time with a twist. A couple of busloads of students are moving toward The People's Consultative Assembly building. The interesting part is that there's a group from Bogor demonstrating not *against* but *for* the government! I'll give you a call if it gets interesting!" Which usually meant when things started to go berserk.

Jailudin entered the four-story shop lot, located in a redeveloped city central super block. He rented his floor from the owner of the Sundanese restaurant on the ground floor, who also leased the second-floor to a direct-marketing company that sold children's books. Jailudin's office was on the third floor, a simple outfit managed entirely by his secretary Rosa, the assiduous Chinese girl in her mid thirties, unmarried, devoting almost all her spare time attending to her one true love, the Bethany Church.

When he entered, Rosa signaled to him that someone was in his office. He arched his brow and gave her a wondering look.

"A lady from some human rights group," she whispered.

"What's she want?"

Rosa gave him a shrug. Taking his sweet time sorting through some incoming mail, while making an attempt to figure out who his guest might be, Jailudin was in no particular hurry to enter his office. In these *reformasi* days you never knew who could be waiting for you behind the door. While the term freedom was easily tossed around, it had never truly been tested. And when push came to shove, the government reverted instinctively to its old trait: they started to abduct people. Half a dozen students were still reported missing since the May riots.

"You must be Jailudin," a slim woman dressed in brown pants and a black blazer, brightened as he entered. "My name's Rafida."

Jailudin walked round to his desk. There was the usual

shapeless pile on his table that seemed to take on an abstract art form as the day progressed.

"How can I help you, Ms. Rafida?"

"I represent an independent body called Association for Women Against Rape, or AWARE. We need a photographer…"

"Ms. Rafida, I'm a photojournalist." It was always safe to turn down any solicitation for help. He had to watch what he was doing. For all he knew this could be a trap that would incriminate him in sedition. Anything could happen in these days of uncertainty. "I don't shoot group photography," he said with finality.

"I understand, Mr. Jailudin." She slid her body forward, her face set with self-assurance.

"Please allow me to finish," she said and then paused as if to let her words sink in. "It had come to our attention that you are a reputable news photographer. You are exactly the kind of person we need to help bring light on the shame that this nation has incurred on its womenfolk."

Those were acrimonious words that rang out from a very angry soul, Jailudin thought. He twitched his nose as if in anticipation for a surprising whiff of a soul-cleansing scent or at the very least, something, anything other than the bland, unflavored generic void. God, what would it take to bring some scents to his nose?

Life had been quite good to him. He monitored his powerful FM transceiver, tuned to the national intelligence frequency, searching for his lead every day. He took to his regular round when something erupted, captured the struggle, the rampage, the wreckage, and ultimately the bodies. Then he sold them to the highest paying bidder. Nothing to it! A straight transaction. Good pay for a job well done. Much like any other profession. Why in the world should he jeopardize everything for a cause that was doomed to failure? How did anybody think the military could clamp down on dissension in this country of two hundred odd million people for the last thirty over years! Why, they could do the same thing over again, *reformasi* or not! The bloody military…hastily he pried open the Venetian blinds and peered anxiously down the street.

"I'm sorry, Ms. Rafida. I only do the hard news. You know, the breaking news. I don't do the investigative type. It's too demanding on time. Really not my specialty."

"We fully understand your concern, Mr. Jailudin," she gave Jailudin a reassuring nod as if acknowledging that she knew fully what he meant. How devastating that look, that little twitch of the head that seemed implicitly to suggest a thousand accusations.

"If you are inferring that I might be scared off by the government. I'm afraid, you're very mistaken."

"Not at all, Mr. Jailudin. How could I be so impudent

as to suggest something of that sort? I'm referring to the matter of monetary recompense."

Jailudin's face turned instantly crimson. What a smart aleck! First, she accused him of being a coward, now she was suggesting he was a mercenary. She insinuated all this without even using a single word to that effect.

"You will be paid in full, with an additional payment upon completion of your assignment," she paused for effect, then matter-of-factly, "In dollars, that is!"

"Ms. Rafida, I'm sorry if I didn't make myself quite clear. My schedule's really tight. I'm afraid this is too good an assignment to be spoiled by desultory efforts. I'm sure it deserves better handling by someone with more time in his hand. Good day, Ms. Rafida!"

Jailudin rose from his seat. Her temerity was beginning to gall him. There were a million things to do. The last thing he had in mind was to be entangled in something of this nature. It was a losing fight. Any fool could have seen that, but of course not this tenacious little twit who seemed to refuse to budge.

"Do you have a sister, Mr. Jailudin?" she turned on him a piercing look that simply would not want to be brushed aside.

"Yes," Jailudin answered, somewhat uneasy with the growing tension.

"Please understand that what you're about to commit

to will have a lasting impact on her and her daughter's life."

"I can understand what your organization tries to achieve, but as I emphatically stress to you Ms. Rafida, this is not my kind of work. If you like, I can introduce you to someone who can do one hell of a better job for you than I ever will."

"We prefer that you take this assignment, Mr. Jailudin, for a reason. You're an internationally known news photographer. Your photography will automatically be considered genuine. Thus, save the time for verification. This will save our organization plenty of lead time in our solicitation for help. We need all the time we can get to help fellow Indonesian women from ever suffering the atrocity like what happened to them in May."

"Let me think about this," Jailudin said. He knew too well that the determined crusader would never leave his premises without a hint of hope. "I need a couple of days to consider this. I'll...I'll let you know."

Jailudin felt like kicking himself on his behind. He must have sounded like a self-serving prick.

Ms. Rafida rose, straightening the crease on her pants, before reaching out her hand, "I have full confidence you'll come around, Mr. Jailudin. Because what you're about to do is for the greater good of all women in this country. For that, *that alone*, is enough reason to take the assignment."

Perfect. The unnecessary stab of guilt! Just what he

needed by way of celebrating his birthday. A lightning strike of conscience to rejuvenate his jaded soul. When he showed her out the door, Rosa, who, as always, had listened to every word that was spoken inside his room, gave him a scalding look that verged on scorn.

"How could you refuse her?" she glared at Jailudin when he came back.

"What's with everyone today?" Jailudin shook his head and flailing his hand in the air he trod into his office.

Later at the Captain's Bar in Mandarin Hotel, Sheryl, who had somehow claimed the place as one of her favorite haunts, posed the question, "So are you going to take the job?"

"I don't know, Sheryl. Too risky! I just don't trust these clowns in the government. They'll never let these women get anywhere near the truth. They'll squash them like flies." With that Jailudin quaffed down his glass of Bintang. Wiping the suds from his mouth, he said, "Why the hell should I be involved in something asinine like that?"

"Maybe you'd want to do it for the spirit of the fight?" The lilting question mark at the end of a statement, that trademark of American idiosyncrasy, never failed to drive Jailudin up the wall.

"What fight?" he said, glancing around the pub that was beginning to fill with late afternoon strays. He felt strangely restless. The coolness from the purring air-conditioner could not calm him down. He thumped the beer glass on the bar. "Nobody wanted the truth to come out. The government sure as hell doesn't want people to know they were involved, that would influence their standing with IMF. The Indonesian people, oh, they're innocent souls. They live in sheltered reality. They believe nobody, least of all Indonesians, is capable of such atrocity. It's in their very nature: they're the most good-natured, subservient lot you have ever met."

"Don't do it then! Nobody's putting the screws on you here!" Sheryl swiveled around, staring at Jailudin in mock anger. Then with both her hands flapping, she broke into a clucking chicken noise.

Jailudin shook his head with disgust, and then gulped down his second glass of Bintang.

Randy, Jailudin's man on the streets, burst in through the door, squinting frantically around.

"Yo Randy," Sheryl waved at him.

Randy made his way through the crowd and wedged his thin body into the small space between their stools.

"J, you've got to come with me, now," he said. Beads of perspiration flowed down from his slick forehead.

"Slow down. Buyung, get him something to drink,"

Jailudin said.

The bar tender shoved across the bar a glass of ice water. Randy snatched it and gulped it down. Water sloshed down from the corners of his mouth onto his sweaty cotton shirt. "Something's going down in the university!" he said.

Jailudin put some money down on the bar and reached down for his knapsack.

"Sheryl, you would want to come with us!" Randy said.

Out on the foyer, Randy stopped and briefed them. In a few hours, the combined forces of the students from three of the city's biggest universities would convene and launch the biggest rally since May.

"Something nasty seems likely to happen," Randy said. "The military must have been tipped off about this. They're setting up barricades all the way to the MPR building."

"Let's go," Sheryl, who had been restlessly idle for the last few days, couldn't wait to get her hand onto something, anything.

They got onto Randy's beat up Wrangler. The jalopy rattled the short distance to the Catholic University, just below Semanggi Overpass. A mass of coeds had started to congregate at the entrance to the university. A bullhorn blared out direction for the newcomers to follow the path marked with red ribbons into the compound.

Jailudin inserted fresh rolls of Kodak film into his two cameras, a Cannon EOS 88, fitted with a Vivitar long lens and his old reliable Nikon. Randy, the deft magician, had somehow secured them three badges, the necessary official stamps to be allowed into the compound. The soldiers watching vigilantly from across the university formed an impenetrable double-line. Nearby enterprising street vendors had taken the opportunity to set up shops.

A platform had been built with makeshift planks and props. A bespectacled young man in a flowing anorak was working the crowd to the chant of *reformasi, reformasi*. The atmosphere warmed slowly to the beat as it gathered emotional force. Then, the student leader, a thin man with a youthful face, made for the stage and grabbed the bullhorn.

"We've heard enough of what they wanted to do for reform. We've seen nothing changed. This government is absolutely useless. It's the lackey to the previous one. It must go!" With that the ground shook with stomping feet and the air was filled with the clatter of irons. "Tonight we'll march to the MPR. We'll take over the building. We'll stay at all costs until the phony president steps down and makes way for a legitimate government!"

Jailudin moved away from the crowd to a safe distance. He pulled his camera out discreetly from his knapsack and started shooting away without flash.

The mob started to move in one direction to the left and like a shifting body it began to form into a knot. In the maddening din, Jailudin could barely make out what all the commotion was about.

"What were they shouting, J?" Sheryl grabbed the sleeve of his shirt.

Jailudin could feel the tremor in her voice. He leant forward and listened hard. "They spotted a military intelligence agent!"

The boisterous crowd immediately fell upon the sturdy man whose disguise in a student outfit looked preposterously in contrast with his fuzzy army crew cut and his wire-tight physique. At first they threw punches at him, then one of the students hurled a rock. The army man stumbled and fell to the ground, cowering under a deluge of blows.

Jailudin clicked away, shifting from place to place for the perfect angle. The army man's bloodied face appeared in glimpses between someone's arm, then abruptly engulfed in a heap of bodies.

A few moments later, there was complete silence. The mass of bodies quickly peeled away, leaving an immobile body on the ground.

The sudden quiet spread like a heavy pall over the campus yard. Then murmurs swelled, at first from individuals to individuals, then spreading like wild fire from groups to groups, and then suddenly exploding into the masses. Loud and discordant, the commotion resumed to reverberate in the yard. The student leader raised his bullhorn. A strident yell filled with as much fear as with bravado prevailed over the hubbub, "For our future, for the future of all Indonesians, we have to do something and we have to do it now!" As if following on cue, the students raged toward the entrance. The anti-demo squad fell on them right away with teargas. Pandemonium broke out. The students, temporarily disoriented by the stinging smoke, moved back and regrouped and then charged again. But this time they were met with flying rubber bullets. The squad forming a two-tier line, equipped with batons, ferociously pressed forward, forcing the students to back into the campus. Meanwhile, heaps of students fell down, trampled underneath the pressing police squad. Shrieks of agony echoed in the commotion. The campus foreground was covered deep with billowing smoke. The students were in disarray, running wildly, knocking each other down.

"Stop! Somebody's shot...he's been shot with real bullets!"

Jailudin pulled back into the compound, clambered up to the top of the front building, clicking away without pause. Sheryl stuck close by him.

"Where's Randy?" Jailudin suddenly asked.

"He's probably gone, J! I saw him with the students a

moment ago!"

"Randy!" Jailudin called out, but his voice was lost in the engulfing madness.

Just then the student leader raised his bullhorn and shouted, "Stop! Stop! Stop!"

But it was too late. Raw emotions had gotten the better of both sides. The situation had gotten out of control. Knots of students were strewn everywhere on the campus yard writhing in agony.

"Time to go, Sheryl!" Jailudin pulled Sheryl's trembling hand away.

"How about Randy? We can't leave him here!"

"Don't worry about him, Sheryl. He knows how to take care of himself. Come on!"

As they were dashing toward the back of the campus, Jailudin brushed sideways against a woman clad in the familiar Red Cross garb. She turned, her raven hair resplendently flowing. She gave Jailudin a brief apologetic look and then she was off, scampering away with the first aid kit in one hand, toward where the students were groveling miserably on the campus ground.

For the first time in so many years, Jailudin caught a fresh whiff of the breeze; it smelled of a mixture of the poplar trees and the briny air heralding imminent rain. It was brief, yet tantalizingly enlivening like the promise of a reprieve.

Jailudin, stricken like a gaping fool, stood absolutely motionless, unable even for a moment to wrench his eyes from the lithe, fleeting figure that was gradually disappearing among the crowd.

They cleared the campus ground through a hole in the fence used as regular passage by the students.

"J, I don't think it's safe out here, stay over at my place tonight."

They hailed a taxi, one of the few that was still plying the city for fare. The cab driver took a clear look at them before stopping to pick them up.

Sheryl's place was in a ten-floor apartment tower tucked away on a byway, away from Sudirman Road, built during the economic miracle banner years. The tenants consisted of mostly rich businessmen's mistresses and a few expatriates like Sheryl.

"If you are ever in need of a companion, look no further, this is the place, J!" Sheryl said as they ascended on the elevator to eleventh floor. "I have never seen so many fabulous women. They're so...so glamorous. But I'm sure three days out of the week, they're so, so very lonely!"

"Why, Sheryl, you sound exactly like a pimp!"

Although her apartment was furnished, it looked bare and unlived in. Aside from a rucksack tucked in a corner of her bedroom, a mountain bike leaning against the wall of the sitting-room, and a laptop on the desk, there was hardly any visible moveable or immovable object in her room.

"Pretty minimalist, isn't it?" she said, throwing her keys onto her bed. "Like it this way. I can move in and out without too much fuss about what to carry or not carry with me! Can't really bother with life's unnecessary attachments!"

"An apartment is too much of a luxury for you, Sheryl. A storage space would do just as well. And think how much money you'd save!"

"Keep your opinion to yourself. Anyway, make yourself at home. I'm taking a shower!"

With a steaming cup of coffee gently cradled in his hand, Jailudin pulled a chair by the window. Outside in the parking lot, the rain was drumming on the tops of the cars and pelting at the windowpanes. From inside the bedroom, Jailudin could hear Sheryl furiously tapping away at her laptop.

He watched the wisps of steam coming off from the coffee in his cup and dissolved out into the night through the gaps beneath the windowpane. How scintillating the aroma must be, he wondered. The thought gave him an unexpected lift. What woud Arabica or Robusta smell like?

Then the tapping stopped. Sheryl emerged from her room wearing a jersey and a pair of shorts.

"Look at you," she said.

"What?"

"You look so much like that…that famous bending, thought laden sculpture."

"Rodin's Thinker?"

"That's right. You're it."

"Oh, stop," Jailudin said.

"What's bugging you?"

"I was just wondering how long all this nonsense is going to last!"

"What's going to last?"

"The demos, the rhetoric, the brutality…"

"Do I detect a note of sentimentality creeping in the soul of the pro?"

"It's just so senseless! It's like a nuisance that refuses to go away. Nobody in this big and sprawling country has a clue where we're all headed. The students with their ever-changing agendas for reformation, the politicians with their incredulously silly punditry, and the bureaucrats…forgive them they are so inept they haven't got a clue."

"What do you care?" Sheryl took a sip of coffee from Jailudin's cup. "You're a professional. You take pictures as they take place, and then deliver them to the world. Let the rest of humankind make the judgment. We're only a couple of pencil pushers and photographer."

"It's easy for you to say, Sheryl! If something big takes place in the Philippines tomorrow, you pick up and go! I'm not going anywhere, you see!"

"Same difference, my friend! We can't afford to get involved any deeper, or we won't be doing what we're doing, we'll be rallying with those students!"

"What made you decide to 'do' Indonesia?"

"I wouldn't miss this for the world! Outside of a major shift toward democracy in China, this is probably the biggest test of democracy in the entire Pacific Rim! If it works here, the next countries will be Malaysia, Myanmar, Cambodia...I'd love to be able to witness it unfold in the next twenty four months!"

"What if it takes longer than that!"

"It either will happen in the next twenty four months or it won't ever happen in this decade. In which case, the country will be pulled apart by disparate forces. There'll be a whole lot of stories to tell, in any case!"

"They're stories to you, aren't they?"

Sheryl turned and took a good steady look at Jailudin. "Don't take me for a heartless hack, J! I've seen worse things in different parts of the world. I've shed tears, risked my life, lost the people I cherished most, and in the twenty years I've been doing this, I've seen this happen over and over and over again! It's inevitable. It's evolution. Nobody can prevent it. Who am

I to think I can change things around the world! I can only observe, analyze and present a situation from its truest and most honest angle and then move on to something else."

"I'm sorry, Sheryl! I didn't mean to upset you..."

"It's all right, J! I understand."

For a brief moment, they peered out the window into the damp darkness, perplexed by the sudden flareup.

2

*M*ayLin had a terrible premonition something ominous was in the making to wreck her plan. She could feel it in the way her eyelashes bat with such ferocious prescience. The tireless hours toiling in the confined quarters of the AWARE, Association for Women Against Rape, to put together a charity event that was to raise enough funds to support rape victims and create programs for prevention. A long-delayed dream project that would involve distinguished personalities from a cross section of religious and cultural backgrounds. Everything was so close to reality and yet it could be so easily ruined with but one word from a single person: her father, the great LeeAng.

A titan, both in the physical sense as well as in his standing in the community, LeeAng, although fondly known outside of the family circle as Uncle Ang, was nonetheless unremitting when it came to family ground rules. His cardinal rule was to stay away from politics. This was an uncompromising given, which was not exclusively only for his immediate family but extending to his closest associates as well.

It wasn't so much bucking the system that worried MayLin; it was what came with it. The hardship tale of his early beginnings, which he never tired of recounting whenever he needed to straighten one of his children on the way of life. With a finger crooking under his chin, his mind started to wander off into the far-off nostalgic past, when, he would proudly tell her, he single-handedly built his business empire from scratch. And how he had been able to achieve all this with his honor intact, his conscience clear and his hands free from politics.

Like most Chinese Indonesians of his generation, he had emigrated from China when he was in his teens. He had journeyed with Uncle LuSook, his father's youngest brother, from a small province in Guangzhou, trading their way to Batavia. He had proven to be a fast apprentice to LuSook. Before the age of fifteen, he had helped LuSook establish themselves as the dominant players in the commodity trade. His sense of fairness and his kind-heartedness had endeared him to the farmers. Over time, with closer ties with them, he had been able, after LuSook's death, to branch successfully into property development, and from there on there was hardly anything to hold him back. With the same unwavering integrity, he had mobilized his businesses, growing bigger and bigger each step of the way, initially into agriculture, multi finance, then moving to telecommunications, and before long he had built a business giant, which he named GrupAstrix.

Now, with reform and the ensuing push for affirmative action, the pressure was heating up on successful Chinese businessman such as LeeAng, who had been accused of building his wealth at the expense of the lost opportunities of the *pribumi*, the indigenous.

MayLin dreaded the moment when she would be forced to divulge her plan to him. It was just a question of time because she had intentionally included his name in the list of distinguished patrons. She knew him well enough to know that if she hadn't placed his name he would probably think of it as a nuisance, for after all it was for a good cause. Stubbornly, however, MayLin had insisted on putting in his name. She had wanted people to know that while the Chinese might seem indifferent to the point of negligence to social events they had done so not out of choice. They had shied away not because of lack of conscience or generosity, but out of insecurity to venture out, out on a limb, being put on a spotlight. For years, they had been forced to eke out a life, albeit, through perseverance and thrift, a successful life, it was nonetheless one that was carved in absolute insularity by distancing from public involvement.

MayLin, raised and educated by choice locally, had thought it was time for his father and his ilk to come out and get their rightful place in the community. Little did she know how her youthful reasoning was to cost dearly to his father's otherwise unperturbed existence.

But now she had a project to realize. And when she had her mind made up, there was hardly anyone who could stop her. Her mother had excoriated her hopelessly that she had too much of her grandmother's boorish determination, an ungainly trait that was so very unbecoming of a Chinese girl.

But then that was mother. Dear old mother, she would never understand. For her, MayLin's place in life would forever be at home, dolling up for the most eligible suitor. And the men, the men that mother and her aunts would like to see her betrothed to, oh, they could hardly keep up with her stride, let alone with what she had set her sight on in her life.

First things first, she had to bring Uncle Tuts, his father's most trusted head of finance, into her camp. She had, on various occasions, with a touch of her charm and plenty of twisting in the arm, had her way with him. The portly man with a weakness for roast chicken moved slyly away as soon as he saw MayLin approaching him with a beguiling smile.

"Uncle Tuts!" MayLin's unctuous greeting almost caused the piece of fried chicken to pop out of the old man's mouth.

"What is it you want this time, Missy? "

"Nothing, Uncle Tuts. What a wonderful Moon Festival party!"

"Ah…yes," Uncle Tuts said, eye askance, unconvinced by MayLin's sudden appreciation of tradition.

"I've always loved the lanterns, the fireworks, and…" at this, she grasped his hand, and whispered, " …and food, food enough to feed a whole village of destitute families! Food for bedraggled little boys and girls! Food to nourish newborn babies! Food for mothers who need to breastfeed their babies! Food, Uncle Tuts, is something these people never have enough! And we shamelessly have in surfeit!"

"Why do you always have to make a case out of nothing? This is Moon Festival dinner reception, my child. Your father has to show hospitality to his distinguished guests and colleagues."

"And the impoverished are left shaking in hunger, just a few blocks away! I find it difficult to develop an appetite for dinner, don't you, Uncle Tuts?"

"What's bothering you, my child? Come off it!"

Sensing a ray of hope in the inscrutable impassivity, MayLin hugged Uncle Tuts, who appeared absolutely flustered by so much unusual compassion.

"Now…that's enough! I haven't promised anything, have I? Oh dear, what kind of mischief you're about to get me involved this time!"

MayLin told him her plan. She could see Uncle Tuts's blood slowly drain from his face with each detail. By the time she was finished, he looked pale as a cadaver.

"You can't do that, MayLin. He..." he said emphatically, "He will definitely not approve of this."

"Why, I don't suppose we need to involve him, do we? In fact, we needn't bother him with such trifle!"

Uncle Tuts shook his head despondently, as if a heavy burden had just been placed on his shoulders. "This time you're going to get us into trouble. Big trouble!" he muttered endlessly.

The guests that made the list of her father's invitation each year were invariably business associates and colleagues from his office. And they stayed mostly within the cloisters of the main hall. Outside, everywhere, in small clusters in the garden, sitting on the hewn rock seats around the water lily pond, or chatting, loitering about in the kitchen, were Mother's guests.

Unlike their modest appearances on a regular day, they were dressed for the occasion. The jade bracelets with gold trimmings, the sparkling diamond earrings, the triple-tier sapphire necklaces and the fashion, the outrageous fashion, fit more appropriately for slimmer figures, was forced wholesale onto the grotesquely plump bodies. Each year, MayLin took in the laconic scene with hilarity.

From the corner of her eye, she could see they were closely following her every movement. Aside from the opportunity to parade their outrageously glamorous togas, MayLin knew why the Moon Festival reception was always such a hit among the mothers.

It was the game of matchmaking, which was what ultimately kept their interest and which was the sole reason they attended the reception. And it was the prevalent topic of conversation that got them all intrigued and unaccountably exhilarated. The son of so and so had the poise and charisma so very suited for MayLin. With MayLin's intelligence and dynamic nature, the son of so and so, being the more patient sort, would just be the right fit. They chattered away annoyingly as if she was a cattle head about to be called up for a livestock auction.

She had always looked on the bustle with disdain and avoided at all costs to be accosted by any one of the mothers for even the briefest chitchat. Over time, she had devised various curt but polite expressions to excuse herself:

"My goodness, Auntie Lee, you do look so splendid! Aha, there's my kitchen maid, I think I'm going to go chop up some limbs…oh you know, for my medical experiment!"

Or when she was not in such a fantastic mood to dispense with humor, she would cursorily remark, "Auntie May, you must excuse me. I think I'm about to get really sick!"

She discovered that grace and propriety were the two most overrated virtues of the Chinese civilization. She rather thought they were to be blamed for helping to foster the gossipy nature of so many rich and idling Chinese ladies. At this, she was about to take a turn and make one of her famous disappearing acts into her music room upstairs when a hand touched her lightly on the shoulder.

"Where do you think you're going, young Missy?"

"Grandma!" she brightened at the benignly grimacing old lady.

Grandma Miranda, her maternal grandmother, lived in the old colonial house left by MayLin's father when they moved into the new house. No matter how hard they tried to talk her into moving, she simply wouldn't budge. She said she enjoyed the solitude, the ample space to potter around in, the sun-drenched patio with her potted plants and her collection of large-print romantic books, twittering birds and a couple of Pekinese. Oh, who would trade all that for the little corner in the new house. No one had ever dared underestimate Grandmother's sheer force of will.

"What a surprise, Grandma. This is hardly the kind of occasion you'll enjoy!"

"You're right, Missy. I didn't come for the silly reception. Never liked it and never will. So inappropriate!" she held on to MayLin's hand, tottering gingerly along the gravel path in the garden.

MayLin was anxiously biding her time. Grandmother was never known for small talk. Even when MayLin was a child, she would rock her speechlessly in her lap the whole afternoon until she fell into a complete peaceful slumber. And she rarely ventured out of her comfortable abode. If she didn't come for her father's reception, she must have come expressly for a purpose.

Sure enough, before they reached the end of the garden footpath, she stopped at a wooden bench and pulled MayLin down to sit by her side.

"You know, Grandma never liked meddling in your affairs..." she paused, her forehead wrinkled as if to gather focus for her thought. "But with the riots and the uncertainty, it's no longer safe, Missy, to be wandering about by yourself!"

"Oh, you worry too much, Grandma!" MayLin said with a breath of relief. For a moment there, she was worried Grandmother was about to make some earth-shattering announcement. "I know how to take care of myself!"

"Listen to her! She knows how to take care of herself," she muttered softly to herself. "What nonsense! You can hardly fix your skirt. Whenever your mother told me you went to town, it worried me sick!"

"Don't worry a thing, Grandma. I'm always with friends. They'll take care of me!"

"Child, you can't go on living like this by yourself.

I notice both your mother and father are too preoccupied to worry about their little daughter!" she said this with a trace of sarcasm.

"I'm fine, really!" MayLin laughed.

Grandma Miranda gave her scant a look as she raised herself gingerly and with one hand leaning on MayLin's hand, she padded on back toward the house. When they reached the back door, she said simply, "Maybe it's time someone took care of you properly, Missy. Listen to Grandma, for once. The sooner, the better!"

MayLin stood quizzically by the front door, watching Grandmother driven away in her white Nissan into the humid twilight. Her brows arched, she unconsciously lapsed into an old habit of hers: biting her thumb. She couldn't figure out what prompted Grandmother's enigmatic appearance and just as puzzling the unusual conversation.

"MayLin, did I see Grandma here just a moment ago?"

Mother appeared radiant with good humor, as she always did on such occasions. The sweet talk, the royal homage, the copious compliments she received from her obsequious friends, all that was more than enough to turn the most guileless woman puffy with pomposity.

And when MayLin told her she had already left, she said, "That was so very like Grandma! Barging in and out unannounced..." Her face, then, brightened when she saw her friends, who could hardly wait to trade yet another piece of enticing gossip, wave furiously for her to return to their fold in the garden.

When MayLin returned to the house, the guests were leaving. Except for a few people chatting lightly by the bar, the room was quite deserted. As she made her way toward the staircase, she passed the study room. Through a small opening in the door, she could peer inside the smoke-filled room. Father was ensconced in his regular brown leather chair with Father Santoso next to him and Haliman, the successful owner of a large distribution company, facing the other way. There was somberness in the way the words were spoken and the long pauses that ensued.

Following the prayer call that resonated through the city's minarets, the day broke in through cracks in the grubby shades of Sheryl's apartment. She glanced quickly at her well-traveled digital alarm clock by her bed. Half past five. The sky was gray as lead. Sheryl rubbed her eyes, barely able to ward off the drowsiness from her fatigued slumber.

Immediately, she saw the note left by Jailudin. A quickly scrawled note saying he would meet her for a drink later in the afternoon. With both hands clasped behind her head, she contemplated the streaky early morning sky framed in her window. It was like staring at a trompe l'oeil painting. Ever shifting and changing, it never remained the same. The true colors were forever elusive. Sheryl studied the mesmerizing patterns with the intensity of a fortuneteller delving into tea leaves to decipher unwritten secrets of fate.

To the locals, she was just the *bule*, the foreigner, who seemed to have a quiet appreciation for the indigenous irreverent sense of humor. Always observant, spoke very little, constantly scribbling away on her little notepad. Somebody who never even thought for a second about crouching down with the guys at the various roadside stalls for a cup of *kopi tubruk*, the people's regular choice of unsifted coffee. And those in the press corps who ever got near enough to her marked her as the unfailing American, with all the prerequisite characteristics of the American can-do spirit, which was just as well because it saved her from cumbersome explanations. And she, on her part, played the role to perfection.

She was one of the guys, the dynamic operator with no time to sweat over the personal asides. Yet something gnawed at her this morning as persistent as a gnat. The clamoring thought knocked about in her head, refusing to be brushed aside.

It was Jailudin. The peculiarly taciturn man, hardly the sort she was familiar with in the press corps. But there was something in the reticence, in the stillness that seemed to foreshadow a much profound and complicated nature. Something in the impassivity which seemed to keep casual trespassers at bay. Over the past few months, she had grown used to the unwavering presence, the one constant figure in the whirling world they hurled themselves into daily. But no matter how hard she tried, she could hardly discern much behind the generous smiles and the overwhelmingly generous deeds and gestures.

After a couple of mismanaged personal mayhems, too many and too painful to keep a straight count, Sheryl decided to leave home, leave the country altogether, and, she hoped, forever rid of the intricate matter of attachment, of men, and the unpredictable games called relationships. She sternly reminded herself she was not about to commit another flagrant mistake in that department.

But then again, she consoled herself she could always pick up and go. Just like what Jailudin accused her capable of doing. After all she had built enough credibility over the years to be able to pick up a new assignment almost anywhere in the world. All she needed to do was pick up the phone and leave for, say, Cambodia the following day, and have another crack at starting her life over. She penciled in a few notes on the blank part at the bottom of the cover paper and then faxed the freshly finished article to the editor of Herald Tribune's Asian Edition. When she finished, she grabbed her backpack and keys and left the apartment.

She had plenty of time to kill before meeting with Jailudin. What grueling and exciting events awaited her, she wondered. The prospect held a certain inexplicable allure that she thrived on a daily basis.

She turned round the corner toward Dunkin' Donuts. There was time when she could hardly believe that the country was in such a dire strait financially whereas malls were packed, supermarkets were swarmed, restaurants had a queue, even a small outlet of the fast-food chain like this one was crowded. She was held up in line for quite a while for her regular order of munchkins and a cup of black coffee, then made her way toward a seat in the far end of the restaurant.

Bomb scare and more stories of looting, the headlines on her morning copy of *The Jakarta Post* heralded. In one instance, the plundering act happened right under the president's nose. As soon as his entourage left the Sunday Market where he had visited on his safari round to survey the availability of staple food and cooking oil, hundreds of villagers fell upon the well-stocked stalls, beautifully displayed for photo-ops, and tore the place apart, pilfering everything in sight.

She flipped mindlessly through the pages. An intriguing piece caught her attention. Mysterious occurrences of food packages being dropped at villages in the outlying areas of Jakarta had aroused speculations that a philanthropic hero had emerged. From the way he chose the places for the distribution of his aid, which consisted primarily of small villages in fine religious environments, it was wildly speculated by the convinced few that the benefactor was a very rich *ulama*. Others speculated that the deposed president, with his billions plundered from the state's coffers over a thirty-two year period, suddenly struck by conscience, was making an attempt to redeem himself. While others, who looked on the charitable deed with skepticism, warned of insidious motives veiled behind the kind gesture, considering that the unaccounted for generous deeds followed so closely to the killings of religious leaders. Meanwhile, recipients of the charity made flowing statements about their personal encounters with the benefactor. They described him as prophet-like in benignity, while others reported that they saw bright lights illuminating the villages. As with most rumors, once kindled, spread like wild fire.

A scuffle at the entrance brought Sheryl back to reality. A group of wild-eyed youth, carrying a scythe, a samurai sword and rusty daggers, were scrimmaging with the security guard at the entrance. The place plunged into chaos as tables were overturned, chairs flung onto floor. Children started to bawl while men and women tried to make a break through the windows.

Meanwhile, the youth terrorists, the city's new breed of anarchists, the same pack that hijacked vehicles on toll ways, held up trucks and charged into shops and restaurants in broad daylight, easily overcame the security guard and now, brandishing their weapons, moved in toward the frightened crowd.

Encouraged by the terror they inspired, they lashed out, slashing and cutting their way in, forcing everyone to relinquish their possessions, watches, wallets, jewelry into the grubby cotton bags in their outstretched hands.

Then one of the restaurant attendants, enraged by the intrusion, charged out from behind the counter with a fire extinguisher and started spraying at the intruders. The crowd cheered him; some of the more daring men came to his aid. There was a sudden tumult as the intruders, wiping the suffocating foam from their faces, made their final attempt to keep the growing recalcitrant crowd back, but they, either too determined in their new-found strength or too terrified to halt, refused to back down. The intruders were finally beaten back. Hands raised high to shield themselves from repeated blows, the intruders finally let go of the cotton bags, spilling the contents all over the floor. The intruders, badly mauled and bruised, took advantage of the confusion created by the ensuing scramble among the crowd to retrieve their looted possessions, to flee away.

Sheryl found herself shaking uncontrollably. She stood petrified in a corner, barricaded behind a stack of chairs, trying hard to gather herself. She had witnessed worst atrocities, more aggravating and inhumane. But they were somehow premeditated, wickedly plotted and executed with cold calculations by vicious minds that took place mostly in wide-open places with thousands of participants. Usually on the news, they were reported as public rallies, street protests or a massacre.

This was different. This was fresh violence, out from the cold, in abject isolation. This was a wide-eye, random violent act that took place abruptly, with no more urgent reason other than out of hunger, out of sheer despair. It was primeval in its instinct, blatantly outrageous in its force. She was struck, for the first time, by fear for her life.

Where was the land of smiling faces, the unmistakable image of hospitality heralded on the leaflets printed by the government tourism board? The benign people that were once so selfless in their nature and so forthright in their service, they were enslaved by the Dutch colonialists for over three hundred years. It was as if by a single stroke of misfortune, they turned into ferocious monsters and nothing was to be the same again.

Sheryl gathered up her backpack and exited the restaurant. The streets suddenly appeared ominous, enfolding shady characters in the shadows chafing and waiting for the opportune moment to spring out from their hideouts to pounce on unwary travelers.

3

*F*rom the rickety wicker chair in the back yard of his sister's house, Jailudin stared at the gray monstrosity. It looked almost finished. With sunrays glinting off the jutted beams, and creeping ivy vines plastering along its walls, seen from an angle from where he was seated, it gave the impression of a perfectly built house. It was anything but finished. In fact, it was not even three quarters finished when the monetary crisis hit the prices of mortar, bricks and timbers. After countless recalculations of the costs of constructing what would be a long-planned two-story townhouse, Jailudin found the price too steep for him to carry on the project.

It had become a daily ritual nowadays for Jailudin to plant himself in different spots in the backyard each morning. With his papers and cup of coffee, he sank into the wicker chair, shifted into a new position and proceeded to stare abstractly into the massive structure, trying hard to visualize, from a different aperture of perspective, the imaginary house resplendent in its finished state.

In reality it stood despondently in its ramshackle ruined state, an awkward testament to a dissipating dream, now a communal property to pigeons, bats, a bevy of ducks and God knows whatever crawling creatures that had found shelter in its many shady hollows.

"How long has it remained in this way?" he asked his nephew, Ronny, a bespectacled nine-year old boy who had grown quite attached to him since Jailudin decided to move temporarily into his sister's so as to oversee the construction of the house. When construction work was finally halted, he had intended to move back to his old apartment, but month after month slipped by so swiftly that before he realized he had settled in, unknowingly integrated into the family.

The boy looked up from one of his series of comic books, and myopically said, "Almost six or seven months, Uncle J!"

"Maybe it's time we did something about it," Jailudin said.

"What are you going to make of it, Uncle J?"

"Oh, I don't know, maybe tidy it up a little!"

"Whatever for, Uncle J!"

"At least, it won't look so…so useless, like a garbage dump!"

His attention completely diverted from his comic

book, the boy now followed Jailudin's gaze and contemplated the mammoth structure. He said after a while, "Will still be a dump!"

"Ronny, time to have your lunch!" It was Fatima, Jailudin's only sister, calling shrilly from inside the house.

Ronny picked up his comic book and shambled reluctantly back. Moments later, Fatima came out from the house, blinking in the sunlight.

"J, you really worried us. I just can't understand why you couldn't at least give us a call to let us know where you were," she chided, loosening the strings on her apron. Then, a smile, just as briskly as her reproach, came on her face. "Happy belated birthday," she gave him a hug and a kiss on his cheek "We've got plenty of cakes and food prepared for you from yesterday."

There was a gap of at least seven years between Jailudin and Fatima, but there were times when Jailudin felt almost like a kid brother with his overprotective sister. Ever since their parents passed away a couple years ago, she had somehow taken over their mother's task of taking care of Jailudin.

She was a successful art director at a multinational advertising firm before she got married to Rizal and decided to let go of her career in favor of raising a family. Jailudin had always told her it was a great shame, wasting all that talent to become a domestic help. She had laughed at Jailudin, saying what he knew about raising a family when he didn't even know how to get a girlfriend.

Those were the heady days of success and ambition, when Rizal was the promising marketing manager drawing incredible salaries at one of the deposed president's sons' automotive venture. Entrenched in a mountain of debts, complicated further by investigations from the Justice Department on allegations of misappropriation of funds through the government banks, the company was finally foreclosed. Rizal suddenly found himself unemployed. He had tried to find a new placement ever since, but to no avail, because there was really no urgent demand for a marketing manager in such a lackluster market.

Of late, he seemed engrossed in the study of the Qur'an and spent long hours helping to tutor the neighborhood children at the mosque.

The flurry of daily preoccupations about the house, what with taking care of Ronny and Katya, the youngest, all of which couldn't conceal signs of anxiety that began to reveal underneath Fatima's eyes. Those eyes which once shone with such confidence and gaiety.

"Sorry to have worried you so much," he said. "I was held up at work. Too late to try and get back, so I stayed over night at the office." He had to lie because telling her that he had stayed over at Sheryl's would have definitely provoked questions he couldn't even begin to know how to answer.

"How's Rizal keeping?"

"It's tough going for him, but he seems to be coping well."

Jailudin could detect the uncertainty in her tone. Equally he could see it in the slight slouch in her steps, the little hesitant gestures, the distant look in her face that it had been hard for her to adjust to the sudden change in their lifestyle.

"If this drags on, it'll be tough going for everyone!" he said.

They stared in silence at the bulky nonentity as if the answer to the burning question of their trouble lay deep in its dark recesses.

"You should do something about the house, J!"

"Funny you should say that! I was just telling Ronny about that only a while ago!"

Fatima shook her head, as if flicking off a pestering thought, and turned back toward the house. Jailudin called back to her, "Hey, you know you can always count on me when you need help!"

"Thanks, J! We manage quite fine," she said feebly, almost inaudibly, as if an unbearable strain was taking all her breath away.

Now, what am I going to do with you, you big bulky gray block of nothingness? He mused, trying hard to figure out a way not to let the gray monstrosity go to waste. He tried turning it this way and that in his head, but the image of the ideal house kept slipping away from him.

There had been naturally an inexhaustible amount of suggestions from every quarter. Solicited or unsolicited, from the maids to the gardener, everyone seemed to have an opinion.

"Build a bird's nest house," the old gardener suggested. "One kilo of the precious swallows' nest can sell easily for millions of *rupiah*! A fabulous income in these hard and unpredictable times, don't you think?"

"Turn it into a greenhouse," the maid chimed in. "You can grow organic vegetables: tomatoes, alfalfa sprouts, long beans, green pepper…Or better yet, grow orchids, lots of beautiful orchids, yellow, white and red. Oh, they'll be so precious!"

"Clean it up and turn it into a place for sholat," Rizal suggested solemnly. "We need a proper place for worship."

These thoughts turned intensely in his head as he ransacked his brain, mulling over all the possibilities.

At least once a month, Rosa made it a habit to walk the extra few blocks to the Children of Christ Orphanage from her house, a semi-detached two-story house she shared with her parents in one of those heavily populated real estate developments in West Jakarta. For as much as she could, she tried not to miss her visit. It was a habit that she had assiduously cultivated for years.

That evening, after work, she was seen carrying a sack bulging with clothes and toys, all of which she had gotten by begging, wheedling, even forcing out of friends in her neighborhood and from people she ran into in her office.

That night, however, she failed to make the last block to the orphanage. The nuns, who had expected her visit, later told the police that they had waited for her until half past eleven when her mother called and found that she hadn't arrived. The police had been notified, a report immediately filed, and the neighborhood security corps alerted. Her friends, mostly from the Bethany Church, relatives and colleagues had one and all been contacted, all with no result.

When Jailudin received the phone call from Rosa's father, he was at the Captain's Bar with Sheryl who was taking quick successions of peppermint shots while recounting the tale of her horric encounter with terror.

At first, Jailudin thought Rosa must have gone on one of her regular prayer rounds at a friend's house. It was a regular event among the believers who usually made their round at night, so as to be able to gather enough participants after work and prayed for a friend's old relative's or parent's recovery from, usually, an impossibly terminal illness.

But when on the next day, he discovered that she hadn't

showed up for work and was told on the phone by her tearful mother that she hadn't returned home, Jailudin knew he had to do something, real fast.

He made his first call to Randy, but no one picked up the phone. He then called Trian, one of the guys Randy hung out with. He had no clue where Randy was; in fact he was still pissed off with Randy because Randy had stood him up. They were supposed to have met at a pub in the city the night before.

Jailudin had asked for Trian's help to get in touch with his myriad connections with the district's underworld characters and see if he could get any information. Then, he called up his friends in the press who were on hospital beats. The final call that he made was to a dear old family friend, the retired Police Chief, Syafudin. The least ambitious career policeman who, however, commanded the respect of the rank and file of the Central Jakarta Police Force. He had once jokingly told Jailudin that he had mistakenly sidetracked into civil service for lack of peer pressure. His parents were both successful surgeons in the army hospital, his sister was an orthopedist and his brother a dentist. In Syafudin's view, there was really nothing challenging out there for him that either his siblings or his parents hadn't already done better. That realization simplified his life. He cursorily picked a career in the police force, easily passing ranks until he found himself promoted the City's Chief of Police, and discovered to his chagrin how cumbersome and political the position he got himself into. He began to lose interest fast. He was marking time in the last few years he was the *Omnipotent Chief* until pencil pushing work and endless parades in the sweltering sun completely spoiled his sense of humor, and started to bother his mental health. He took the early retirement package and never gave it another thought.

"I knew there must be something you need from this old geezer whenever you call," he laughed heartily.

He had lived next door to their house, a friend to both his father, who was a golfing partner to his last day, and to his mother, who pampered him with gourmet dishes and her fabulous jackfruit crepes. He remained a faithful bachelor throughout the years, indulging himself on his golf games and fishing trips. Jailudin was this little gopher that meandered in and out of his house, the beloved son that he never had.

"Uncle Syafudin, you know I wouldn't bother you if it wasn't for something really urgent!"

"I know, son! I'm only jabbing at you. By the way, when are you really, really going to settle down with some nice lady?" he said.

"Looks like we have the same fate, Uncle Syafudin. Always on the wrong side of bliss."

"You're on the wrong side of your senses, my young buddy. Quit talking nonsense. Tell me what's the express purpose of this phone call?" he said, turning all at once serious.

Jailudin told him the full story. When he finished, there was a long pause. Syafudin asked him a few questions, mostly details about Rosa. And that was all. He told Jailudin to call him back in a few days.

When he put the phone down, Jailudin saw Sheryl huddled in the sofa, eyes widening, gazing anxiously at him. "Will they find her, J?" she asked with a tone that verged on pleading.

"I don't know," Jailudin said. The uncertainty was ripping him apart. "But I promise you we're going to find her!"

He sank his face down on the desk, a mass of desolation. And for the first time since she knew him, Sheryl had a glimpse of the man behind the placid façade. Later, she couldn't remember what prompted her hand to reach over and tenderly pat at the back of his head. Just as blurry, how the hand then curled gradually round his neck into an embrace.

In the moonless night, two unidentified Hino trucks, freshly painted in camouflage army green, with their headlights doused, rumbled through the rutted tracts toward the village. About two miles off the main gate, the trucks came to a momentary halt. Then, trundling off into opposite sides of the muddy path, they disappeared behind the cover of thick shrubbery.

Darkly clad figures took turns disgorging from the trucks. They rode down the ramp on motorcycles, strapped with leather pouches filled to the brim with packages of instant noodle, coffee and different sizes of cans containing condensed milk, sardines and chicken soup. They moved briskly but steadily, well rehearsed in their strides, disciplined in their movements.

When the whole team was properly saddled up, the leader signaled off the first dispatch. This was followed at five-minute intervals by another dispatch until the complete squad was sent off, each into a pre-assigned direction.

It was a hamlet of approximately sixty or eighty families, an hour and a half from the City of Jakarta. Cruising through brambles and thick foliage that overshadowed the residences, scattered at irregular distances on uneven terrain, the team of dispatchers seemed unfazed as they mobilized with familiarity from one shack to another, undeterred by low visibility. The packages, all packed in similar sizes, were cast off in conspicuous spots in the verandah or hung on the branch of a tree by the gate of each hovel.

They plied back and forth until every last packages in the trucks were delivered. Before the first crack of light, they started heading back to the clearing where the trucks were. The leader swerved his bike to the side, and started clicking off his counter as one by one the motorists rode up the ramp, back into the trucks.

First light was streaking the city skyline when the trucks, relieved of the load, rattled their way, clanging and banging out of the laterite paths on their way toward the city. Soon, the peasants would start their day. They would rise and rub their eyes. When they opened them, a miracle would occur. An incredible act of tremendous generosity had just been enacted. The vittles were probably adequate sustenance to last for at most two to three days, a mere whetting of appetite for these desperately destitute people, but what they brought as a gesture was something far more lasting. What they brought was the brightness of hope, an outreaching hand that pulled them up and set them on their feet, the humbling first steps toward something good.

The thought brought a satisfactory sense of achievement to the man, whose smile was hidden completely behind the muffled disguise.

4

When MayLin saw the company around the breakfast table under the overarching branches of the gigantic oak tree, she knew this was no ordinary morning family gathering. There was Father at the head of the table, looking primly commanding in white shirt and tie. Mother, nestled by his side, looked sheepishly out of place. It was as if the solemnity of the occasion was too much of a burden for her fragile psyche. But the telling sign of trouble materialized in the person of Uncle Tuts. Unless on very urgent calls to get Father's approval or signature on certain JV documents or to report crucial decisions drawn by the board of directors, Uncle Tuts was hardly a regular presence at the family's breakfast table. As she approached the table, she gave him a look that burned menacingly with explosive tantrums. Uncle Tuts, with his head bent, took a keen interest in the floral design of the tablecloth.

"MayLin, sit here," Father motioned her to a chair near him.

She slithered into the garden chair, surveying the dour faces around the table. Mother's makeup was cracking under either the immense humidity or the unbearable tension. Uncle Tuts had a blank expression on his face. He was fiddling with the spoon in his soup.

Father finally broke the silence, "MayLin, Uncle Tuts told me your plan to organize a charity event." He spoke slowly, picking his words with great care. "I thought it was a commendable thing to do…but given the rather uncertain situation, it would…it would be in my opinion a slightly risky thing to do."

"But, Father, this is not about politics! It's not about taking risks. There's no risk involved in being a decent human being. It's certainly not risky reaching out to these women, poor unfortunate women who have been brutally violated, to help them get up on their feet, regain their dignity!"

"Yes, I understand how you must feel, what with the time and effort you put into this thing," he had meant to sound understanding and sympathetic, but the words that came out of his mouth seemed unfeeling and stiff. "I'm fully aware of that. But, you see, you needn't overextend yourself in such a way. You can always help by making your contribution anonymous. It's always been our way of doing things. You don't need to go to all the trouble of organizing such a messy event!"

"MayLin, you should listen to your Father," Mother chimed in. "In fact, I really haven't a clue why you got yourself involved in this sort of madcap. This doesn't become a proper lady at all!"

"This is precisely the reason why we should do something about it, now. Because that's exactly what everyone is thinking. Stay out of trouble. It's none of our business. But think about it just for a second, Father. Unless we do something to show our good intentions, they're going to take away whatever God given rights we ever have!" She punctuated her words in the air with the bread knife, her voice hoarse with spontaneous emotions.

"My dear, nobody's saying what you try to do is wrong. We're just saying that it might not serve us well, especially if you put me down as a co-sponsor of the event. This is not the way we do things around here. We never expose ourselves! Never!"

"Go on then, live the subterranean life of an illegal immigrant. Wait for the next millennium, and maybe, just maybe, by then everyone will be friendlier and more acceptable! This is the chance of our life! This is the time to be taken seriously, to be counted, and to be once and for all accepted."

"Don't be so naïve. Things are never as simple as you imagine them to be," Father sighed, keeping his temper in check. Who could he blame if his daughter turned out to be just as headstrong as he was!

"Never mind!" MayLin shoved the chair back, getting to her feet.

Mother was busily dabbing the tears that were welling up her eyes. Father, struck by the sheer obstinacy, watched speechlessly, as MayLin strode away, insouciantly defiant to the last tilt in her gait.

"Who was the girl I just talked to a moment ago? She can't be the little daughter who pulled at my shirt just the other day," he sighed. Then realizing he wasn't alone, he regained his composure. "Uncle Tuts, send someone to follow her. See to it that she will be protected and stopped from getting herself involved in anything silly!"

Father shook his head, his brows frowning. He looked as if he had just aged a couple of years.

"Please, Uncle Tuts, make sure nothing happens to her," Mother reiterated, imagining the cozy, picturesque little world she had grown so attached to for so long now disintegrated steadily around her.

As soon as she got out of the garden, MayLin rushed to her Honda Genio, parked by the shed on the left wing of the mansion. She slipped into the car, turned the ignition key and with a determined push of the automatic lever, she drove off, kicking up a trail of dust behind her.

Instinctively she knew that unless she did something soon, Father, with the tentacles of his influence and connection, would see to it that her plan would forever be unfinished. He would never hinder it in any conspicuous way, but things would somehow never get done, the completion would forever be delayed, set back oh, maybe, a few weeks. She knew him well enough to know that when he said no, that was it. It was the last word, unmoved by pleadings, feigned tears, or even the gentlest persuasion.

She pulled out the cellular phone from the handbag, and made a few phone calls to the handful of people who had been the mainstays of the organization since its inception. She called for an immediate conference at The Center.

Rafida was overjoyed. It was an unprecedented emotion, considering the barriers, the insurmountable obstacles she had to get through day after day after day, to beg for a handout of help. Help from finicky celebrities to endorse the cause. Help from reluctant government officials to reopen the rape cases from the May riots. Help from frightened rich businesspeople for cash contributions.

There were times in her most vulnerable moments of dejection she wondered why she, Rafida, the frail, and unwittingly helpless creature, should bother. In fact, nobody in her family quite understood what she was striving to achieve by the way she threw herself into her work, day and night, unflinchingly, one disappointment after another. For them, her concern seemed to have been misplaced. There were more urgent miseries in the world to cry her heart out for. How about the illiterate *pribumi* children, the little urchins that loitered at street junctions, hands outstretched, sometimes panhandling, but oftentimes street robbers in disguise, pinching side-view mirrors from cars waiting for the traffic lights to change in the intersection.

Instead, she wept and turned sleepless over raped Chinese women. At first, they figured it was one of those sudden flashes of conscience that would just as suddenly evaporate. But how grossly mistaken they all were. She didn't just become more engrossed in her pursuit; she sank herself into it, unconditionally. The pain and suffering she encountered in her daily contact with the rape victims enraged her, empowered her with the drive, the single-minded focus to pursue the culprits and bring them one and all to the court of law. The rebuffs, the subtle threats from the military, the mockery by skeptics who until this day insisted that the May mass rapes were hoaxes, mere fabrications of the unknowledgeable few were more than enough troubles to drive off even the toughest man. Instead they instigated in her a sense of purpose. A burning sensation that throbbed in her veins daily, imbuing her with a sense of direction that she had never known she was capable of possessing.

To save time commuting back and forth from her house, she had put herself up at the small office they rented above the dry goods store in an obscure part of *Kota*. On this particular morning, she was overjoyed because finally Jailudin, the famous photographer she had tried so desperately to recruit, called her. He didn't initially call to offer himself for volunteer work. He had called to ask for her help in tracking the whereabouts of his personal assistant, Rosa. But Rafida, by tweaking and prodding the terribly despairing man, had eventually succeeded to turn him around; at the very least she had got a commitment from him to visit the Center for further discussion. It was a joyous moment of triumph. It was like a crack of light breaking through the cloudy sky.

Rafida was savoring her little moment of victory when MayLin's call came through. Before she could blurt out her incredible achievement, MayLin broke in breathlessly, "Rafida, we need to meet. Something just came up. We need to speed things up or our project will never pull through! I'll see you in about twenty minutes! Get everybody."

Seizing the opportunity, Rafida called Jailudin and asked politely if he would mind coming to the office *now*. To her astonishment, Jailudin said yes.

Another thing that buoyed her spirits this morning

was a mail that came in this morning. It contained a letter of certification from the United Nations' Commission on Human Rights. With the official recognition, AWARE now became an internationally sanctioned organization. It was the long-awaited seal of approval badly needed by The Center to protect itself against any future infringement from the government. Rafida felt immense relief seeping through every pore of her body. Perhaps, now she could do something good.

When the search became prolonged, it began to dawn on Jailudin that Rosa might have vanished. She could have been killed, her body thrown away in swamplands near the airport or some god-forsaken places. The thought made his skin crawl. He gritted his teeth, thinking and thinking hard, which was all that kept him busy nowadays. Nothing else mattered. What could have pricked his interest more than hunching over a map tracing and retracing the paths that Rosa could or couldn't have taken, forever looking out for new ways or new insights, something that may have been overlooked, to crack the case and safely reclaim Rosa. The poor girl, she would have been contented just devoting her time to the orphans, her religion and her overwhelming sense of responsibility for her work in the office. For the last six or seven years, the quiet, soothing presence was like a safe haven for Jailudin in the best or the worst of times.

Now she was gone, without a trace, like a wisp of vapor abruptly dissolving into thin air. At first, the unexpected turn of event confused him, and then as it began to sink in, he felt infuriated by the senselessness of the whole affair. Of all the people in the world, why did it have to be Rosa, he kept repeating to himself. She was probably the most decent person he had ever had the privilege of knowing closely. She radiated kindness. Warmth and generosity came off her as naturally as an aura, as easily as a breeze.

He made several attempts to reach Randy, but somehow the man seemed to have disappeared from the surface of the earth. When he finally got hold of Trian, Randy's friend, he could hardly get a morsel of information out of him. By the way he slurred his words, sliding and traipsing the syllables, it didn't take Jailudin long to find out that Trian was tripping.

It was with a great sense of relief, moments later, when he found out from his colleagues on hospital beat that there was nobody fitting the description as faxed by Jailudin checked into hospitals in the last forty-eight hours.

Meanwhile, there was no news from Uncle Syafudin, not a beep from the old man, which was rather unusual, considering his sundry contacts and his mercurial temperament that had a tendency to drive him into frenetic impulses. But as it was, the curmudgeon for all he knew could have gone fishing and got drifted away in a big sea storm.

It was out of desperation that he finally made the phone call through to Rafida. He was at his wits' end, having no idea where to go to get started in his search. So when Rafida called back to ask him if he could make it to the Center, he was only too glad to respond. Sheryl, who had been just as badly affected by this, offered to come along with him. It was just as well that Sheryl came along because when they stepped into the small meeting room at AWARE's, he saw to his dismay that he was the only male in the room, backed wall to wall with female participants.

There was something in the way the room was decked out that made it seem to exude with so much femininity. Maybe it was in the way the pots of purple geraniums were placed on the table, symmetrically hung on the wall, artistically nudged in on the window ledge or maybe it was the cream and yellow floral wallpaper. But on a closer look, he discovered distressing details creeping out from unobtrusive corners of the room. There were newspaper clippings on the rape victims, blown up poster size, terrorized eyes peering out through the inky smudge of enlarged pixels. Then, there were the pictures, of women captured in different facial expressions and postures. They stared out of the bookshelves, from end tables, from the small spaces between the windows, like so many reminders of promises not fulfilled.

His eyes fell on the lithe woman that had come to him like an apparition on that chaotic night of confrontation at the university. Then it started again, the strange and indescribable sensation. His nasal tickled irritatingly as he felt a maelstrom of scents rushing in, spreading through his entire being. He snuffled voraciously, drawing in fresh breaths like a newborn suckling its first taste of milk from its mother. With the oxygen circulating in his brains, he experienced a sudden rush of giddiness that totally loosened his muscles, prompting him to fits of uncontrollable sneezes.

"God bless you," the woman spoke to him, a surprising gesture that took Jailudin by surprise. A smile, big and confident, beamed on the serene face as she sidled gracefully toward him and offered him a small packet of Kleenex.

"Oh thanks," he said, gladly accepting the succor. He was struck by how easy going her nature was and how forthcoming the way she carried herself.

"I'm MayLin," she said. "And you must be the famous photographer everyone so eagerly waits for!"

"Please, enough of the embarrassment," Jailudin said huffily, mopping his sniffling nose, unable to fight off the profusion of scents that ceaselessly inundated his nose.

"We're truly grateful that you make yourself available for us," she said, the sincerity in her tone caused Jailudin's heart to skip a beat.

Rafida went up to the lectern, tapped lightly on the microphone. The jarring feedback reverberated through the room and soon the murmuring voices died down.

When Rafida was making her opening speech, MayLin briskly whispered to Jailudin that many of the participants were parents or relatives of the victims. Although they had been harassed constantly by anonymous phone calls, warning them not to make their cases public, they had nonetheless come forward, courageously filing details of the horrid acts. Jailudin surveyed the harried faces, worn out by fear and eyes glaring with pent-up emotions. Every wrinkle on the distraught faces carried the burden of a story, a tragic story, which was rendered more tragic because the legitimacy of their stories had been denied.

"Today, our center has been fortunate enough to be graced by the presence of a man who would greatly help us in our efforts. My colleagues please welcome Mr. Jailudin!"

Jailudin acknowledged the reception by nodding his head shyly. The sisters clapped their hands and stomped their feet.

"Now, the next order of things," her voice trailed off, citing a list of recent achievements. A number of suspects linked to the military had been detained for further interrogations. The Ministry of Women's Affairs had approved to look seriously into allegations of rapes. At the closing of each cited achievement, the sisters repeated the ritual of clapping and stomping. There was a brief moment of disruption when suddenly an old woman in the back row burst into tears, calling out repeatedly the name of her lost grand daughter. There was a bustle as the women clamored around the old lady, showering her with words of comfort and commiseration.

When the room finally settled down, Rafida resumed, now in a voice laced less with confidence than deep sorrow. "As you know, we have planned to organize a fund-raising event for quite sometime. After serious deliberations we've decided to carry on with the project and hopefully stage it immediately. I'll now pass the microphone to the project officer, my colleague, MayLin."

MayLin took over the mike and in a reassuring voice she unveiled the plan for the project. Her voice lilted with excitement as she described what would be the first and the biggest charity event ever organized in the country. It would be a splendid evening of education on the plight of raped victims, veiled cleverly with programs of cultural dances and ethnic music. When she was finished, the sisters again gave their approval by clapping their hands and stamping their feet. She asked for everybody's prayers and assistance to make it happen. Before the participants left the room, she called for those who would like to volunteer to leave their names on a form by the table near to the door.

"I hope you'd join us, Mr. Jailudin," she said when she returned to his side.

Jailudin gave her a sheepish, noncommittal smile as he glanced at Sheryl who was absorbed in a conversation with Rafida. He suddenly remembered what Sheryl once told him about keeping himself above the fray, maintaining a professional distance. Then, he gazed at the row of pictures. Rosa's face could easily be peering out from any one of these pictures. The thought discomfited him terribly, causing him a great pang of agony.

Rafida was in the mood for celebration. When all the guests had filed out the door, she suggested that they go in MayLin's car to a small restaurant nearby. Over dinner, Rafida talked profusely about the brightening prospect of the Center, now that it was fully sanctioned by the United Nations' Commission on Human Rights. And with the support from Jailudin, the synergy would be an incredible boost for the Center. She paused every now and then to emphasize her words. The light-hearted frivolousness vanished from her face, replaced by an air of businesslike seriousness. "We still have a long way to go," she said. "We hardly scratch the surface of the matter. The facts about the rapes need to be validated, before vindication can be accomplished. And more than fifty women in different parts of Jakarta went through the shameful atrocities, but to the world it's a *maybe*, or *allegedly* fifty women.

Nothing was for real. The facts are daily shifted, manufactured to the whims of the bureaucrats. People no longer know the truth."

Her words whizzed by him like the pleasant buzz of background music in a hotel lounge. He was seated in the corner of the booth, having a hard time concentrating. Every part of the sensory system in his body was reveling in unfettered freedom, cavorting in the transcendence, in the liberation of his olfactory system. The world floated by with such lightness, everything he lay his eyes on appeared covered in an ethereally surreal patina. He was suffused with a wonderful sensation that seemed to portend of infinite possibilities.

His eyes, like the sensitively sharp lens fitted to his camera, drank in the smooth and silken skin, the angular bone structure, the beautiful neckline, the tiny strands of hair flailing freely as she excitedly illustrated to Sheryl an amusing piece of anecdote. His eyes were enslaved, his senses indentured, hocked to the last sensation to one person, the one person no farther than a seat away from him. An absolute stranger until a few hours ago, a blot, a nonentity in his memory databank, an unregistered blip of emotion in his heart, now she seemed to take over, taking everything, lock, stock and barrel, in hostage.

Helplessly, feebly, he watched her engaged in an intriguing topic with Sheryl. He made an effort to conceal the thumping heartbeat, the revolting internal turmoil, and smiled timely whenever in the midst of her excited confabulation, her eyes, those beautiful orbs radiating so much light and intelligence, flicked naturally toward him.

The vibrating buzz from a cellular phone, Rafida's StarTac, brought a semblance of reality back to his frazzled senses. Rafida flipped open the receiver and listened, and as the furrow on her brow deepened, the conversations stopped.

"When did this happen? I understand. I'll meet you there right away," she said, flipping shut the receiver. When she looked up, all eyes were on her. "That was Karlina, she called from the hospital. One of our sisters has been assaulted. She's in the St. Carolus Hospital now," she announced with gritted steadfastness.

The trip to the hospital, St. Carolus Hospital across from the University of Indonesia's old campus, seemed to take forever. Silence, once allowed to wallow in its own morass of lethargy, bred an unbearable awkwardness, which in turn became convoluted in its inertia until, with elapsed time, all will and urgency to break it completely evaporated.

Jailudin stared at his feet, there was a part of him questioning loudly what he was doing there, scurrying in a vehicle to the hospital to see a woman he hardly knew, whereas he should be spending time searching for Rosa. Another side of him, the side that he was unfamiliar with, told him to go with the flow, let the constellation of events define itself, and prayed that there was a plan in the way things turned out.

And then of course, the undeniable impulse from the innermost of his being, ever goading and pushing, a budding sycophant which gladly subsisted on the faintest hint of a smile, the subtlest gesture of intimacy. He basked in the glow of these thoughts, roaming freely in a gilded journey that hurtled beyond the confines of reason, past the borders of commonsense. In that split second, he felt as if he had been struck with the wand of a fairy and suddenly blessed with a radiant lucidity that rendered the stubbornly obtuse and abstract clear as broad daylight.

What he saw next in the small whitewashed room, whose floor was reeking of generously poured disinfectant, curtailed the unfettered flight of his imaginations, and propelled him into the abyss of human iniquity.

LeeChin, a waif-like child in her early twenties, fluttered like a leave, legs drawn up, her hand grasping tightly on the head of the bunk bed. Her eyes, the only visible parts of her face not swathed in bandages stained with spots of blood, depicted the indescribable horror.

When she saw Rafida enter the room, she broke down uncontrollably. Rafida held her tightly in her bosom. Tears trickled down her cheeks, as her body shook with the spasms from the girl's outpourings. All of a sudden, the desire to find out the truth had lost its urgency. Nothing else mattered. The sight of the sobbing girl was sufficient explanation; words would merely blaspheme the sacristy of the moment.

Later, words would flow from the tremulous lips. At first, in stuttering incoherence, then as the girl regained some sort of composure, words both thunderous and piercing spewed forth with fierce vehemence.

It had happened at around six thirty just as LeeChin was entering her house. She had gone on a fact-finding trip to the house of a recently raped victim in Sunda Kelapa area. She could have collected the details she needed in a few hours; instead she spent the whole afternoon keeping company with the victim until she fell asleep. Then, she took some snapshots of the various parts of her body that was badly mauled with swelling bruises. She was groping for her keys in her handbag when it happened. She hardly felt anything. There was a thud against the back of her head, and all lights went out of her. When she came to, she found herself splayed, with both her hands tied to the backseats of a moving van. Two men masked and crouching beside her, stared at her, their eyes glittering with squalid intent.

"This," the squatty one warned, tracing the serrated edge of his navy knife on her cheek, "...this should teach you a lesson not to meddle in matters off limits."

"And..." the thin man bent down and ripped open her blouse, breaking off her buttons one by one until her bras were revealed. "...If this is not clear enough, maybe this will always refresh your memory!" He took the navy knife from the squatty, ripped off the support strap and in one swift move he cut off her nipple. She shrieked and blacked out. When she was revived, she was in hospital; her body and face were swathed in bandages. She was numb from the anaesthetic.

Sheryl fought back the tears that were threatening to burst through the wall of her defense. She looked on defiantly, hands akimbo. She wanted to remember, to remember every detail, to capture and etch the moment in her memory. Making it an inseparable part of her, so that one day, with furious vengeance, she would unleash it back to the world, letting this burden of her heartache, this agony of her soul, be shared by one and all.

Rafida sat like a statue by the bedside, grasping the girl's hand. The ensuing calm filled the room with the languorous emptiness of spent emotions and fatigue. The sight was too unbearable for MayLin; she rose to her feet and slipped out of the room.

Jailudin watched with fidgety discomfiture as the heartrending revelation unveiled before him. He had great difficulty pinpointing the exactitude of his emotions. There was never a doubt that he felt outraged by what had happened to the girl. There were moments in the midst of the girl's utterances he could even feel a palpitation in his chest. But as if a mechanism was built in his system to keep a constant check on his emotions, he found himself slowly burrowing back into his old shell of cozy disengagement, returning to the familiar environment of unattached aloofness. He felt relieved when he saw MayLin leave the room; discretely he rose and made for the door.

Outside on the street, MayLin was leaning on the back of her car, both hands digging in her pockets. Her eyes languid, she looked blankly at the busy traffic. When Jailudin joined her, she made an indifferent acknowledgment by moving aside to make room for him. Both were swallowed in an unfathomed depth of silence, as the city's bustling traffic fleeted by.

Jakarta had the relentless look of an unfinished piece of impressionist painting, dabs of colors in bold strokes, impulsive and unpredictable. There was no linear symmetry in its architecture, nor harmony in its colors. It strained the eyes just to keep the disparate elements in focus. And the noise was unforgiving, an incredulous concoction of discordant sounds, banging, clanking and rattling, a ceaseless racket constantly abusive to the eardrums.

Finally, she turned her head, eyes brimming with tears. She grabbed Jailudin's shirtfront and then buried her face in his chest. The mask of restraint was off. The superficial surface of unperturbed calm disrupted, she was unleashing the insurmountable burden of grief, wailing to her heart's content.

Jailudin was flabbergasted, caught completely unprepared in the dubious position of assuming such a staggering responsibility. He held the bobbing, jerking head clumsily, gnawed by indecision the course of action he was supposed to undertake. In the end, he decided to remain still, letting the moment dictate its course.

5

*I*t happened in the blink of an eye. When he opened his eyes, she was gone. She must have gently extricated herself from his arms, climbed into her car and driven off. Just like that, without rhyme and reason, everything went by with an almost dreamlike sequence. He was left dumbfounded, gazing in complete incomprehension at the slowly disappearing taillights' beam.

For a moment, he thought seriously of giving chase. Then he thought better of it. It wouldn't have done any good, he figured. It would only force her into even more drastic measures, like driving herself into a tree or something reckless like that. Besides, judging by the manic way in which she pulled herself away from him, she did not appear to be too keen on being followed for the moment.

Jailudin found himself standing by the curb, puzzling

over what could possibly have just happened. Each time, he came up short of a plausible explanation. It started with *maybe*, then *perhaps*, and started over again with *what if...*

In any case, he didn't know how to tell everyone about what happened. He was too perplexed to go back inside and subject himself to an impossibly wearying line of questioning. Or maybe this peculiar evasiveness could have something to do with the guilty conscience he secretly hid inside him. Inwardly, there just might be a tad of remorse for harboring such outlandishly impure notions of a woman held so dearly in high regard by everyone. He felt like having transgressed into the forbidden terrain. And the worst thing was that she might have seen through all his thoughts and was frightened off by what she saw. So he walked away.

He would not see her again until the night before the charity event.

Meanwhile his search for Rosa had turned up some interesting results. One morning when he showed up at his office, which was in shambles without Rosa, he found a letter with no postmark, no sender's address, perched brightly at the base of his desk lamp. He slit open the envelope and found inside a note, written on the yellow legal pad easily found in his office's drawers, in the precise and well-turned Rosa's handwriting.

Dear Mr. J,

I know my sudden disappearance must have caused unnecessary anxiety over my whereabouts and safety. Let me assure you that I have never felt happier and safer where I am. I cannot explain clearly to you what I'm doing right now or tell you precisely where I am at the moment. Suffice it to say that I'm safe among friends. Please forgive me for the inconvenience caused and kindly show this letter to my parents so that they too will feel reassured.

Yours faithfully,
Rosa

It was brief and formally direct, revealing nonetheless very little. And yet, the turn of phrases and the words chosen were unmistakably those of Rosa's. Later, when Jailudin showed it to Sheryl and Rosa's parents, they, too, recognized the familiar handwriting and were convinced that Rosa had written the note herself.

There was a huge sigh of relief. A moment of jubilation as thoughts of Rosa being alive filled everyone's mind. But this passed quickly as the natural, ineluctable next question immediately cropped up, where on earth could she be then?

The succinct, yet grueling question found no satisfying

answer. Instead, it pierced the bubble of the prevalent buoyant mood, dashing any hint of hope.

Then, unexpectedly, one day, he received a telephone call from Uncle Syafudin.

"Hi there, young fella," his husky voice boomed through the receiver. The old man sounded full of gaiety and sprite. "How's life treating you?"

"Not too well, I'm afraid. Where on earth have you been Uncle Syafudin? I thought you were going to get back to me in a few days!"

"I know...I know...but why, young man, be reasonable, I may have taken more than a day or two tops, but still a decently kept promise, don't you think?"

It took Jailudin a while to rein in his temper. He loathed the flippant banter. He had neither the time nor the mood to be playful. He needed some answers fast. So when he put the question to him, he sounded rather crass, "Well, what have you got for me, Uncle Syafudin!"

"Boy, are we in a cranky mood," Uncle Syafudin piped up, growing more and more impish and impossible with Jailudin's increasing impatience.

"Please, Uncle Syafudin, we're dealing with somebody's life here. Can you spare me a moment of seriousness?"

The old man chuckled, unable to stop himself being tickled by his own mischievous behavior.

"You really crack me up, J!" he guffawed. "See me at the club tomorrow, after 12, sonny!" He was still caught in the frenzy of laughter when he rang off.

Of course, the club referred to one of the oldest golf clubs situated off the interstate to Bogor, a good forty-five minutes drive from Jakarta. The very same club Jailudin's father had belonged to till he passed away.

It was Saturday, not an especially auspicious day to meet someone in a golf club. To begin with, finding a spot to park his car was a problem. All available parking spaces had been parked double tiers and the parking attendant was not particularly eager to help in such oppressive heat, unless you drove a German make car. Then, there was the drudgery of having to negotiate his way through the sweaty, sullen-faced golfers shuffling in and out of the clubhouse.

He found a sofa in the packed lounge upstairs and waited. He must have waited for probably one and a half hour before Uncle Syafudin, his Nike golf shirt soaked in perspiration, face ruddy with the heat, shambled to his table.

"Aha...ever the punctual young fellow," he hollered, patting him on his back.

"Uncle Syafudin, you're late as usual," Jailudin made a wry observation.

"Blame the Korean couple playing ahead of us! Damn slow players. They should be barred from the club," his voice raised to a pitch as he recalled his lousy day in the course. "Anyway, it's good to see you again!"

He sat down and for a while fussed over his golf paraphernalia, the towel, the small Nautica bag for his golf balls and tees, his glove and cap. They were all meticulously put aside before he made an order for a glass of the club's special, Stamina Juice. A concoction of milk, honey and egg blended into milky puree to be served on ice.

Jailudin sat fuming as the old man went through his routine unperturbed, completely in his element, luxuriating in the after game ritual.

"Oh, you're not in a hurry, are you?" he turned, beaming at the puffed up face across the table.

"Not really," Jailudin answered briefly.

He soon regretted the polite reply he had given the old man, because for that he had to wait for another hour as the old man prattled on about his shanks, his brilliant and mediocre play of the day while chewing on his Teriyaki.

When he was finished, he lit up his cigar.

"I suppose you wanted to know about the Chinese girl," he said somberly. Jailudin was waiting with frayed nerves.

"Is she all right, Uncle Syafudin?"

There was a hiatus as the old man took another puff at his Habanos, Montecristo No.4.

"Don't worry about her, J!"

It was cursorily dismissive, in a tone that sounded almost like a rebuff for his rather inquisitive behavior

"But…"

"Please, trust me when I tell you she's fine, J!"

"But where's she? Her parents are worried sick."

"I'm not sure, J! But I know for a fact that she's safe!"

"This is not fair, Uncle Syafudin. I know you know more than that! Don't keep me in the dark like this! I have a responsibility for her safety, you see!"

"I told you she's safe. Now, get off the case, J!"

Uncle Syafudin turned his head away, gazing beyond the swaying treetops to the faraway mountain, immersed in the swirling clouds of his Cuban cigar.

When he noticed that Jailudin was readying to go, he promptly turned around and said as if by way of consolation, "J, she told me to tell you not to worry!"

Jailudin's reaction was slow in coming and when he spoke, his voice was tremulous. "Are you telling me you actually saw her? You…you talked to her? This is just so unbelievable!"

Uncle Syafudin rose to his feet, smilingly shook his head and headed for the putting green.

Jailudin returned to Jakarta as exasperated as he had come. He felt that there was a wall being erected around him, a conspiracy, everyone seemed to know something about the truth, except him. He was in the dark, in a maze of conjectures and speculations.

When he got back to his office, he found Sheryl waiting outside the door, cross-legged on the ceramic floor. By the looks of it, she didn't appear to have fared quite well by the turns of events in the last few days. Her eyes were bloodshot, markedly sunken on a pallid face. The once calm exterior was now betrayed by the disquietude of disheveled hair and crumpled clothes. But something in her stoic manner, in the way she held her head up, with a glimmer of defiance showing in her eyes, made him want to hold her in his arms, grateful for her being there. Instead, he said, evading the lovely but fiercely querying eyes, "She's all right." When she continued to stare at him, he felt compelled to add, "She's fine, really!"

Jakarta could seem starkly cold and uninviting on days when one's heart was disengaged. Uncle Syafudin's enigmatic remarks were still clinging on his memory like a pestering nuisance. Although the news provided a welcome respite to his badly frayed conscience, it nonetheless hounded him daily in bouts of needling curiosity and nagging incomprehension.

But now he was able to resume work. And there was work, plenty of work, both new and unfinished assignments, streaming in uninterrupted from different quarters. It kept him busy and lent him an opportunity to vent his restless, manic energy to good use. But his heart remained doggedly desolate. He had tried ways to distract himself, by going to the movies with Sheryl, going out to restaurants, reading rapaciously thick tomes on chiaroscuro and photography. But his heart ached for MayLin; it pined maddeningly for the engaging smile, for the contagious warmth. And for the relief he felt in his sense of smell that seemed only possible whenever he was in her proximity.

He called up AWARE's office several times, but mostly he talked to Rafida about work for the Center. He helped them in his spare time to compile a photo essay. He was greatly dismayed by the utter ruthlessness. Scenes of cruelty, distressingly more surreal than any imagined acts of sadism, defied the common man's common belief. Unless one witnessed the contusions on the badly ravaged bodies: a monkey wrench poked into the vagina, the anus severely rammed through by a broomstick. Such scenes of horror when recounted to the next person sounded hyperbolic and verged on the unreal, grist for unaccountable amount of debates and oftentimes fisticuffs in places of work, restaurants and at home. They hit him hard. He was ashamed by his own people, by the undeniable fact that unwillingly he was implicated, a culprit in the atrociously shameless act. It was an unequivocal fact that would be written down in the annals of history for the posterity to judge.

It was no longer possible to be a bystander, unaffected

in his adamant pursuit for objectivity so that he could deliver the truth to the world, unbiased. The truth delivered in the sterilized packages of photorealism. To capture these images that clearly cried out for fair judgement and not to be involved in activism of any cause would simply tantamount to blatant exploitation.

His resolve grew each day he came in contact with the volunteers at The Center. He became more empathized with Rafida's single-minded dedication. He understood now where she had drawn her unflagging energy for the care of each of the victim, her sacrifice for the cause. She was like a savior sent down by the good angels to alleviate pains committed by human folly. This wispy, fragile creature with iron will that spoke with a reedy voice.

And somehow his understanding of Rafida allowed him to see Rosa in a better light. He had always had this fixed image of her being stubbornly rigid and inflexible in her faith, resolute in her pursuit for the charitable causes she threw herself in. Now, it dawned on him how in her boring inflexible way she had always been in reality a better and more enlightened human being. The truth pained him, inconsiderably more so when he became aware of her absence.

In all the time he was carrying out his tasks at The Center, he never once ran into MayLin. Whenever he visited The Center, he always anticipated that she would suddenly materialize from behind the door and smiled that unbelievably sweet smile of hers. He never asked Rafida or the volunteers that were seen bustling about daily in preparation for the charity event and they too never volunteered to tell him where she was. He was loath to appear inquisitive by being overly persistent, so he kept silent; the ache in his heart grew inconsolable.

There was something about melancholy and frustration that seemed to draw one to the other. In Rosa's absence, he found himself drawn closer to Sheryl, who had unofficially appropriated a corner in his office and claimed it as her own. Although he never quite discerned what turbulent soul roiling behind the unperturbed appearance, he welcomed her companionship. It was an indefinite source of comfort from which he drew his solace. In her quiet and discreet way, she helped him in the lab drying the prints, keeping the office in a semblance of order.

Most evenings they went out to dinner. He took her to places away from the designated areas haunted regularly by the city's businesspeople. He took her to the fisherman's village in North of Jakarta. Hunkered down underneath the flapping makeshift tent, they peeled steamy crabs and sipped warm unsifted *kopi tubruk*, listening to the murky sea lapping violently against the porous rocks a few yards away.

They talked about work, about the worsening effects

wreaked by the declining economy. They talked about the people, how they had become violent and impossibly incendiary. Anything could spark a riot nowadays. An innuendo, a furtive glance, an irresponsible slant or misconstrued remark could cause the breakout of a massive disorder, creating indelible rifts among various religious and ethnic groups. The city was in slow slither toward anarchy. There were more reports of cars being hijacked, people robbed in broad daylight, clashes, death tolls ringing in every part of the country stretching from Aceh to Ambon.

Tactfully the subject of Rosa was eschewed, which allowed for their conversations to flow freely, unhindered by guilt and chagrin of her absence.

In rare moments like these, Sheryl's face became more animated, the crinkled lines unraveling slowly behind her eyes. There was a humorous gleam in her eyes. She laughed freely. Her movements were less restrained. It was a cheerful sight. It led Jailudin to reflections of fear, how it petrified a person and constricted not only his capacity to think rationally but also limit the pliability of his physical movements. It was so easy to forget in the confusion of the successive events that Sheryl hailed from America, that paragon land of freedom. Only a few months ago, she had lived and breathed a life of unqualified freedom. How quickly all that had changed by the simple act of transporting herself into this turbulent part of the world, to be subjected to a set of new rules, living in totally unpredictable circumstances.

Jailudin felt it his duty to assume the burden of her agony, just as the responsibility for Rosa's safety was his, his alone. For every mindless act committed in the name of his people and his religion, he cringed with terrible shame. Although in most instances, he was as outraged as the next person, he nonetheless apologized profusely for the mind-boggling inanities, as if he was solely to be held accountable for every senseless provocation and every outburst of conflict.

On one such excursion, after a satisfying dinner of fresh prawns and clams, they strolled down the narrow sandy path on the edge of the sea, enjoying the breezy pleasant evening flushed with the radiance of a full moon. They chattered lightly, their voices hovering above the intermittent crash of the waves against the reefs. There was talk of taking a short trip to Bali, away from the city that was becoming fraught with besieging fear. The prospect greatly cheered Sheryl and rendered both pensive with pleasant notions of the sun, the beach and the freedom from always having to look over one's shoulder.

It was in that unguarded moment as their minds wandered that two black jeeps suddenly bounced out of the clumps of palm trees and lunged at them, rubber screeching and thrashing through the sands, stopping abruptly only a few feet from where they were standing. The men that jumped out of the jeeps were clad in civilian clothes, but one look at their upright gaits and their boots showed clearly that they were the militias.

Jailudin stood undaunted, Sheryl's hand held tightly in his, watching these men charge toward them. The leader wearing a red beret shone a flashlight on his face, inquiring harshly, "Are you Jailudin?"

When he confirmed, they pushed Sheryl aside. Two men grabbed him by his arms, flanking him toward the back of one of the jeeps. It took less than five minutes, hardly enough time for Sheryl to stop gasping and let out a cry and they were gone. They had spirited Jailudin away, leaving her shaking in sheer isolation.

It was too shocking. It was like something fresh out of a newspaper article she once read. *A man was reportedly abducted from the beachside restaurant and never seen again.* It was too unbelievably real. Everything she feared and secretly wished to have happen to her, the ultimate fantasy of any roving world-caliber journalist, was taking place right before her. Now she wondered if she truly wanted things to unfold in this way. She wondered if it was worth all this aggravation and pain.

She scurried out of the darkened patch of the beach path, then once on the street she started to break into a run. She saw a taxi slip by and hailed desperately.

Once in the taxi, she drew up both her legs and braced herself. The taxi sped her through clogged streets, shops, fleeting street lamps back to the city. Her eyes fixed ahead on the images rushing through the windshield. She tried to still the involuntary tremors.

6

*D*arkness. The futility of vision. It was intolerably the most vexing inconvenience for any person used to normal healthy vision. It was unbearable because it caused a sense of imbalance, which in turn created a sense of insecurity. Vaguely, through the sackcloth slung over his head, he could discern from the movement of the jeep as it lolled and lurched, dragging from the smooth asphalt path of the city streets to the rugged, jolting tracks, that they were slowly heading out of the city proper. He could also sense hostility by the tightness of his captors' grip on his arms.

"Where are you taking me?" he asked with the desperate belligerence of one helplessly subdued.

The blow, in response to his inquiry, was swift. It came without warning, smashing the back of his head with a resounding thud. It knocked him out of his seat, down on his knees, and rendered him completely senseless.

He had no clear indication of how much time had elapsed, or any idea where he was. When he came to, all he felt was the excruciating pain that spread from the back of his head down his neck and all the way to his knees. Almost immediately after, he felt his muffled face burn with the heat of a halogen lamp.

"Where the hell am I?" he demanded, bracing himself for the unexpected assault.

"Shall we say, you're temporarily our guest of honor," a hoarse voice answered, followed by a burst of snickers.

"Is this how you treat all your guests?" he said sardonically, pointing at the sackcloth over his face.

"Don't strain my patience, Mr. Jailudin or you'd rather I call you J as most people do," he said, intimidating him with the intimate knowledge of his personal background.

"What do you want from me?"

"Depends, Mr. J. It depends on what you have for us."

"I have no idea what you're talking about!"

"I'm sure you do, Mr. J. To begin with, you may perhaps enlighten us on your involvement with The Center."

At the mention of The Center, the pieces of puzzle began to fall into place. Suddenly he realized that these men were some sort of intelligence agents. And by their familiarity with his personal background, they must have spent quite a bit of time hounding him. But why, what could they possibly want from him? He was gripped both by fear and a nagging curiosity.

"I was hired to shoot photography for The Center," he answered crisply, feigning impatience by the tiresome drill.

"What kind of photography?"

"I take pictures of raped victims," he said bluntly with an intention to shock, but there was hardly any trace of emotion betrayed by the man's voice when he pressed on with his interrogation.

"What else do you do at The Center?"

"I'm a photographer, I take pictures and nothing else," said Jailudin, growing quizzical by the turn of the questions.

"Are you sure?"

"Sure about what? That I do nothing else but take pictures, yes!"

A hand smacked him hard on his head. He was stunned by the numbing sensation for a moment as his head spun and the burning halogen light plied back and forth, a swaying vague red orb.

"Don't you get wise with me!" the man thundered. "Just give me straight answers. Now, tell me, are you sure you were at no time engaged in anything else other than photography?"

"Yes, I'm sure," Jailudin mumbled, rubbing the

swelling pain in his head.

"Did you ever notice any suspicious activities?"

Jailudin was about to ask him what he meant by 'suspicious' but he thought better of it, so he answered flatly, "No, never saw anything like that."

As if he could sense Jailudin's incomprehension, the man rephrased his question, "You didn't see any trucks or people moving sacks of foodstuff?"

"Foodstuff?" Jailudin was by now completely lost. "You mean like rice and sugar?"

"Yes," the man affirmed tersely.

"No, but why should I see something like that at The Center?"

The man kept his question floating unanswered. There was a brief pause as Jailudin heard him whisper in consultation with another figure in the room.

Vaguely, struggling in scraps of awareness, he wondered about the man's enigmatic queries. If these were men sent out by the intelligence to scare him off The Center, like the way they frightened off LeeChin and many of the victims' family, why were they grilling him about ridiculous things such as foodstuff? It simply did not make any sense.

Jailudin heard heavy footsteps stomp away from the room. The halogen lamp was doused, which gave his scorched face a welcome reprieve, and the door slammed shut.

With the heat from halogen lamp switched off, the room felt draughty and moist. Curling up his body, he nestled his head against the wall. His mind was wracked by dogged attempts to figure out the riddle. Soon he fell drowsy and dozed off.

In the hazy limbo between the stupor of pain and drifting consciousness, he was splashed with a pail of water and yanked awake. Over and over again, he would be subjected to the drill and withstood the incessant blows of baton crashing against his head, his back and his abdomen.

Sheryl, driven by sheer focus, rushed up the flight of stairs back to the office. Her face looked set with determination as she made successive phone calls. Her first call reached Rafida, who was not unused to unexpected phone calls that brought tidings of ill omen. She listened to Sheryl's shaky announcement before calmly telling her that she would come over.

It took Sheryl a while to find Uncle Syafudin's phone number. She had to turn Jailudin's drawers upside down before locating the old man's home number on a small pocket telephone notebook left on the bottom drawer. She made the call; the phone got through and was let buzzing for a few minutes longer before a gruff voice answered, "This better be good!"

"Uncle Syafudin, this is Sheryl," she blurted out,

fearing that the eccentric old man would terminate the call at a moment's notice. "Something has happened to Jailudin!"

Sheryl's urgent voice and the blurted speech must have shaken up the old man because when he next spoke into the receiver his voice sounded serious, "Hang on there a second, what's happening to Jailudin?"

There was genuine concern and love that could easily be detected in his voice; Sheryl felt a moment of relief as she realized that at least she did not have to carry this burden by herself.

In an uninterrupted spate, she told him everything. When she was finished, catching her breath, she paused. She could almost clearly see Uncle Syafudin's alternating sentiments on the other side, from utterances of shock to annoyance.

"I told him to get off the case! Why didn't he listen? Now, what am I going to do? Oh, for God's sake, I hope they spare him the unnecessary torture," he went on in a tangent, ragging on incoherently as if in a trance. When he resurfaced from his foul mood, back to his senses, he told Sheryl to keep calm and that he would see about what he could do to find Jailudin.

Half an hour later, Rafida appeared at the office. There were half a dozen sisters from The Center stringing along with her. The search for Jailudin had commenced; Sheryl was unofficially made the leader of the search party.

There was no denying that something funny must be going on at the downtown headquarters. This could not have been the handiwork of the city police; it was too neat and too precise in its execution. The stealthy operation, the calculated movements, they bore the unmistakable insignia of the military's special intelligence unit.

Syafudin never relished dealing with these boys. Although there was mutual respect among the rank and file, at least on the surface, these boys seemed to carry with them a haughty air of superiority. They knew, as everyone else who was privy with the way the military hierarchy worked, that no matter how far a career police officer would strive, chances were they would end up reporting to one of them, the commanding officers of the nation's superior forces.

Syafudin trudged through each department in the Armed Forces Headquarters, enduring the bureaucracy and patiently positioned himself in the intersections of hallways, in the labyrinthine maze of nooks and crannies that made up for the warren of administration offices. These corners teemed with cretins of every shape and form: riffraff, hustlers, crooks and go-betweens, plying the offices of the officers for the prized rubber stamp, for a permit or for the precious letter of recommendation that would open up doors to the corridors of ingratiating power and fortune. There was a whole industry of shady, under-the-table businesses transpiring in these hallways, and yet, everything carried on with the unperturbed equanimity of business as usual.

He was at work all the time, trying to get an angle here and there for a scrap of information. He rekindled old friendship, striking up new acquaintances, all the time listening and listening hard for news of Jailudin. But nothing of significance turned up. There was not even a whisper of any kind of undercover activity. In fact, there was a paralysis in these military departments as continuous, unrelenting flare up in many parts of the country had practically choked up the military operations, taken up all available men and zapped all its energy.

He listened to the latest rumors about the scramble for the provision of election funds. Trillions of rupiah were to be dispensed to the established parties. Suddenly, dissension on rules of the imminent general election, debates on the issues of democracy and reformation took a backseat as the priority was given up to how to get into the action, how to carve up a slice of the rich provision funds.

Syafudin, not particularly known for his patience for hubris and casual talk, found himself fascinated by the latest state of corruption. It seemed like only yesterday when everyone was talking so disgustingly about cronyism and collusion, and how these were the ailments of the state to be purged before the country could recover and get back on its feet. It appeared to him that the country was getting on its feet all right, but not because cronyism, collusion and corruption were purged, but because they were put right back on the track to grease the wheels of daily life.

For days on end, these were the hotly traded topics in the hallways. As the days dragged, he grew more and more grouchy and disillusioned by his efforts. There was no progress whatsoever, short of becoming the reigning monger of political rumors in the hallways of the Armed Forces Headquarters.

One miserable afternoon, he was hunkered down in one of the stalls that cropped up like pestering leeches in various niches of the sprawling building. He was contemplating over a tumbler of *kopi tubruk*, not particularly too keen for company, when a stranger tapped on his shoulder.

He turned brusquely and his eyes took in the eager face of a young cadet.

"Can I borrow your light?" he asked timidly.

Syafudin passed him the little torch, which he used for lighting up his cigar. The young cadet turned the gadget with some curiosity in his hand, trying to figure out the way to light it up. Syafudin showed him how to do it. The young man's face lit up with genuine astonishment.

"This is some gizmo," he said, taking a puff at his clove cigarette while admiringly played with the lighter. Reluctantly, he returned it to Syafudin.

Syafudin kept to his silence. He had seen droves of these young men, mostly peasant boys fresh out of high school paying their way into the armed forces and then later paying their way up the ranks. They found refuge in the institution, took pride in the spanking uniforms, the rigmarole of the routine, the fear they inspired on common people, and the potent power in their command. All the wrong reasons, Syafudin thought, to be recruited into the ranks of officers.

But the young cadet was in a chatty mood. He puffed satisfactorily at his clove cigarette, waxing loquacious with each puff.

"It's good to be back," he put his hand on Syafudin's shoulders, striking up an instant camaraderie. "It'd been a couple days of hell out there in the isolation."

Something in the young man's confessional tone pricked his interest. He goaded him along, "So what have you been up to?"

The young cadet nudged closer and whispered, "We've been assigned to detain a man up in the hills of Puncak, in total isolation."

"Who's this guy?" Syafudin asked, keeping the conspiratorial tone so as to keep the young man's confidence.

"Some guy, poor bastard! I bet he peed on his pants," he chuckled. "Being wrapped up in a sackcloth and all."

"What did the man do?"

"He's tied up with some women's movement.

Something called AWAC or something."

"AWARE, Association for Women Against Rape," Syafudin said.

"Hey," the young man turned suspiciously at him. "How do you know that?"

"It's nothing new really. You read about the organization on the paper all the time," Syafudin lied.

The young cadet, embarrassed by his apparent lack of knowledge, laughed and became relaxed once more.

"Yeah, AWARE or shit like that," he continued.

"You care for a cup of coffee," Syafudin offered.

"Yeah, thanks, you're a nice old man," he took kindly to the gesture.

"Nothing to it, my friend. You need to make friends around here. So what unit of operation you belong to?"

"The Phantom Force unit, Army's Special Intelligence Command," the young cadet preened, pausing to savor the glamour of the sound of the title tumbling out of his lips.

"So what was the objective of your mission by taking the guy in? You're trying to scare him off, aren't you?"

"He's scared all right, no doubt about it. You probably wouldn't see him around once we got over with him."

"What, you're going to do him in?" Syafudin asked, feeling suddenly squeamish in his stomach.

"No, man, I meant he'd be scared bonkers to have the

guts to stay in town!" he neighed and thumped his hand, causing the tumblers to wobble wildly on the counter.

"So what do you intend to do with this guy?" Syafudin continued to prod the young cadet.

"The top brasses are worried. They wanted to get to the bottom about the food distribution shit. You know the food packages and stuff. They believe some politician's behind it, there's a political motive," he said the words *political motive* with emphasis to show that he was in the thick of things.

"What's that got to do with this…this man you detained."

"Our sources told us there was someone in the AWAC…"

"AWARE."

"Yes, AWARE. Somebody in there is involved with the Robin Hood thing," he chuckled. Bemused by his witticism, he said the word over and over.

"So was he the man you were looking for?"

"Hard to say. We'll probably rough him up a bit, to be sure, you know. Seems that he doesn't know shit about the whole thing. It's so boring up there, man!" The prospect of returning to the chilly isolation in the hills must have taken the glibness out of his speech because soon he became quiet and sullen with thoughts.

Syafudin finished his tumbler of *kopi tubruk,* paid for both his and the young cadet's drinks, and hurried out of the place. As soon as he got into his car, he called Sheryl.

For the umpteenth times, Jailudin was jolted awake from unconsciousness. He was groggy with lack of sleep and there was aching pain in all parts of his body. He had completely lost sense of time and place. When the steel door swung open and the halogen lamp switched on he sprung up almost like a well-conditioned animal. He sat bolt upright, waiting to be drilled and winced at the expected blows.

Through the miasma of blurred vision, he could discern that instead of the numerous shadowy figures that always seemed to hover around him, there was now only one man in the room. And the man planted himself on a steel chair near him. He pushed the halogen lamp aside, turning it away from his face, up against the ceiling.

"J, you could tell the truth now and be spared the unnecessary aggravation or suffer the consequences," the new interrogator spoke, slowly in a measured, steady voice.

"I've told you everything I know," Jailudin said. He was tired and numbed by the ceaseless drill. His head was buzzing; he found it more and more difficult to keep focus.

"How about MayLin, J?"

He straightened up with alert.

"Who?" asked Jailudin, in a feigned calm tone.

"You know who," the man barked.

"What about MayLin?"

"What do you know about her?"

"Not much," Jailudin answered, cautiously feeling his way around the man's line of questions.

"Tell me what you know," the man's tone was unvaried, levelly disinterested.

"I met her only a few days ago. I really don't know her all that well."

"Think again, J. Think deeply. Do you know of her activities, any kind of activities outside of what she was involved in at The Center?"

"I have no idea. I met her only once at The Center."

"Come on, J. Do not make me use force on you!"

"Screw you!"

There was an eerie screech as the man shifted, dragging the heels of the steel chair forward and lifting one heel, aiming it deadly at the toes of his right foot he plunged it down with the full force of his entire weight. Jailudin groaned, feeling the numbing impact of the steely heels crushing his toes. The pain was sharp and immediate, shooting up excruciatingly like an explosive bolt of lightning from his toes, causing tears to brim over his eyes. For a moment, he was motionless, seized by the searing pain. He was impelled to scream with all his might, instead he grunted, bit his lip, staunchly withholding the ravaging sensation until it slowly submerged into the unplumbed depths of numbness.

"Now, let's start over," the man continued,

unimpressed, pressing down his weight on the heel.

Jailudin fell back, engulfed in a dark, swirling sea of pain. He lost consciousness moments later.

7

When he awoke, in a dizzying blur of vision, he saw Uncle Syafudin's beaming face look down over him. As his eyes reoriented to the light, he began to recognize the faces surrounding him. There was Sheryl, looking pale and drawn, and Rafida, smiling in the cheerful way that she always smiled and a few other sisters, whose faces were quite familiar, from The Center.

"What a mess you got all of us into," Uncle Syafudin said, shaking Jailudin's arm excitedly. There was genuine relief in his tone and hidden joy in the way he kept grabbing at Jailudin. He repeated over and over again, "Thank God we got you back in one piece."

"Thanks, Uncle Syafudin," Jailudin said; his voice was tremulous, hoarse from going parched for days without water.

"Don't you worry about that, young fella," he shrugged

it off, laughingly.

Jailudin knew that for whatever reason he was still alive, he owed it to the efforts of Uncle Syafudin. Only the old fox had the cunning and the wiles to snatch him away from the claws of those outlaws.

He made an attempt to slide up to a sitting position. He groaned. He felt his body crackle with agonizing pain. Sheryl rushed toward the bed, slipping a hand behind him to help prop his back up on the headboard. Jailudin grasped her arm; beads of perspiration coruscating down his forehead.

"Thank you," he said softly.

Uncle Syafudin and the others had withdrawn from the bedroom, now resting and talking lightly in the adjoining room.

"That uncle of yours is really something, J! You're really lucky to have someone like that on your side," she said and went on to relate to him the whole rescue episode.

After gaining the precious information from the young cadet, Uncle Syafudin had called Sheryl to inform her that he had located approximately where Jailudin was kept in captivity. He had told her not to worry and to wait at Jailudin's office for further news.

What he did after that was simply pure Uncle Syafudin's cunning. He made a quick round of calls to his men, those loyal ex-lieutenants who had by now become respectable superiors in the rank and file of city police department. These men were more than obliging to help, especially when told about spoiling the party of some arrogant intelligence boys. So, Uncle Syafudin came up with a brilliant idea, by the pretext of a blitzkrieg operation to sweep druggists around the hills of Puncak, the city police had sent out The Mobile Response Units, fanned out along the hills, turning up every hangout and suspicious hideout.

It did not take long for the men to discover the abandoned shack at the top of an isolated tea plantation. The men had charged into the shack and found Jailudin sprawled unconsciously on the earthen ground, strewn with discarded cans of beer and soda drinks and remnants from the excesses of the men for the last few days. The intelligence boys must have heard of the sweep and did not bother to get into a confrontation, for when the MRU men scoured the place; there was no sign of any of them. The shack was completely deserted.

"They're after MayLin," Jailudin mumbled suddenly, reminded by the urgency of his memory. "We've got to warn her!"

Two hundred kilometers away, in a small town in the vicinity of Bandung, a group of figures, whose faces wrapped in flannel headgear, assembled in the narrow gap between the parked trucks. It was splendid in the wee hours of the morning. A soft breeze was blowing, the air smelled sweetly of burgeoning blossoms. There was an atmosphere of gleeful jubilation as the night's tasks had been accomplished with great success. First light was still a few hours away. There was plenty of time to clear out. They huddled in small clusters, greatly relieved after anxious hours of zipping about like bats through dark alleys and over gulches. They talked in lowered voices, swapping anecdotes of mishaps of the night, like homecoming soldiers comparing scars on their bodies.

The leader strolled among his troop of Samaritans, clicking his counter while calling out names. When he completed the routine, he started to call out for attention.

"Thank you all for yet another night of fabulous charitable work." This announcement was met with a ripple of applause. He coughed softly, waiting for everyone to simmer down. When they finally settled down, he resumed, "There's been all kinds of reactions to what we've been trying to do. Some praise our efforts. Others cast a suspicious eye, looking for a motive where none is there to be found. This should not discourage us nor impede us from continuing to work for charity. However..." Here he paused, allowing a ponderous moment to pass to prepare the group for the gravity of the words to come. "However...precautions must be taken. It seems that there have been attempts by a couple of snooping intelligence agents to pick up on our trails. I can't as yet verify for sure what their express intentions are, but they don't seem particularly friendly." There were cackles and catcalls erupting everywhere.

"I know how you must feel. But always bear in mind we've got jobs to do. And by God, we're going to continue to do them!"

The small gathering came alive with thunderous applause as the volunteers clapped their hands approvingly.

What happened in the next instant caught them by surprise. In their euphoria, nobody saw what was coming. They did not see the men creeping up from behind the tall shrubbery, slowly enclosing the shrouded clearing in the woods where the trucks had been parked out of view. They were also unaware of the slowly encroaching anti-riot vehicles. When on a sudden the whole area was flooded by the blinding beams of searchlights, the volunteers were stunned, blinded for a moment by the sudden brightness, like some nocturnal vermin being flushed out of their hideouts.

"This is the police! You are surrounded. Do not run!" the bullhorn blared as the volunteers disbanded in disarray.

The leader, calmly, held up his speaker and shouted his instructions, "Get on your bikes. Get on your bikes and get out of here! Now!" He kept repeating the commands until he saw that the volunteers made an orderly rush toward inside of the trucks for their motorbikes.

Scrolls of dust swirled up as tires screeched and

thrashed the ground. Wheezing and throttling, one by one, the volunteers mounting their motorbikes shot out of the truck, bounding in different directions into the woods. The police envoy watched, greatly unprepared for the agility and the disciplined way the volunteers made their breakaway.

Within a few minutes, the volunteers were gone. The place subsided, returning to the quiescent state of its former tranquility. The abandoned trucks stood forlornly in their tracks, with their back doors down gaping like the taunting tongues of a couple of churlish urchins.

Sleep was like a seductress's tendril finger, waving at him coyly, luring him deeper and deeper into its tender soporific embrace. In the indeterminate state between fitful slumber and lucid wakefulness, he caught a glimpse of MayLin. She was loping along in the market place, her flowing hair splashing on her shoulders in perfect rhythmic synchronization with her steps. He tried calling out to her but there was not a squeak coming out from his mouth. He grew panicky, and screamed, again nothing. He shoved his way through the crowded path, jostling and tussling toward MayLin's direction. But she was forever unreachable, floating ethereally further and further away from him, until exhausted he stood amidst the passing crowd, following his gaze on her slowly diminishing figure into the distance, her head now and then bobbing into view.

He was startled awake by a refreshing coolness on his forehead.

"So who was it in your dream?" Sheryl teased, as she fussed about him, checking the ice in the compress. "Your face, it looks so beatific. So blissfully peaceful! You must have been dreaming of a woman."

Her hair, which had always been kept short and sassy, had grown a bit. It was now bundled up and tied tidily into a bun so as to allow her to move more freely. Jailudin felt the proximity of her body. He felt the soft curvature of her breast brushing against his cheek as she leant over to punch up the duvet. He felt her waist pressing against his arm again and again. The lingering softness of the skin, the momentary contact, stayed with him, even after she left the room to fetch him some tea.

"How long have I been staying here, Sheryl," he asked when she returned.

"For the last couple of days," she said, blowing the warm tea in the cup.

"MayLin! They're after her, Sheryl! We must warn her," he made an effort to get down the bed, but the paralyzing pain stopped him right away.

She hastily placed the cup back on the tray by the bedside and got up to hold him down gingerly back into the bed.

"What do you think you're doing J? Calm down. She knows J. Rafida has talked to her. They know they're being targeted. They are all taking extra caution in The Center."

Laid up with his eyes idly staring at the flowery décor of drainage stains on the ceiling, he was unaccountably furious by the uselessness of his body, by his reliance on another person for the simplest chore. Days of living by himself had made him adhere to a rigid set of routines that he never strayed from every day. And now being fussed over by another person, albeit by a close friend, was like breaking the code of discipline. Since he had no say over the matter, he kept sullenly quiet.

Sheryl, assiduously, reapplied the compress, tucking him in the bed sheet. Jailudin was struck by how methodical she went about her work and how attentive she was to every detail. A day or two ago he would have considered it totally hilarious if anyone should tell him how the irrepressible American was in fact capable of such tender nurturing.

As if it helped to assuage his embarrassed sense of helplessness, he spoke with stiff gravity, "Sheryl, you might want to consider another assignment."

"What do you mean?" she said, her cheeks suddenly reddening. The question had coincided at that precise moment with her train of thought. It was a gem of a notion flickering in and out of her mind as she was fussing over Jailudin. It was the familiar instinct that had once told her to leave everything behind and flee from her country.

"It's time to move out of this place, Sheryl."

"Why, and miss out on all the excitement? You must be kidding, J!"

"I'm serious, Sheryl. It's no longer safe here."

She liked the way he pronounced her name. *Seereal,* without the *sh* sound. The name tripping out of his lips sounded so droll, so irresistible. *Seereal, Seereal.*

"Come with me then," she said, taken aback by the boldness of her suggestion.

It took Jailudin a moment to digest the proposition. Never in his life had there ever been a moment when he had to face the question of whether he should or should not leave the country. The talk was always more in the vein of getting friends to shift over to reside in this lovely and hospitable country. "Oh, it's a land of such freewheeling opportunities. Anyone with a bit of connection and perseverance could make it out here," the oft-quoted refrain heard so regularly among the people. But there was never, ever talk of moving abroad to live in a foreign soil. The idea once struck him as irredeemably shameful, but now resurfaced by Sheryl's question, it was lent a fresh veneer of possibility. It did not seem such a quaint idea now, he thought, appalled by how quickly things could change. He wondered about the fickleness of time. He wondered how people changed, opinions became hazy, priorities got shifted about and old ideas suddenly turned avant-garde innovations.

"I can't," he said.

"Why not?" Sheryl challenged. "What's there for you here, J?"

"I don't know, Sheryl. I just can't leave."

"It's a whole world out there, J. Besides, it's sometimes good to be away, to look at your life here from a distance. You might be surprised by what you would find once you disentangle yourself."

"Don't change the subject. We're talking about you, Sheryl! Remember?"

"I'm here by my free will. I'm on a mission to capture the shifting paradigm in politics. How about you, J? What's keeping you here?"

Everything, Jailudin thought. Everything he ever held dear was here. The cozy corner in his office, his preoccupation with photography, the occasional drink at the Captain's bar, his sister and the little boy Ronny, these were just as important to him as roots that held a plant to the ground. And everything he ever cherished as worthy of nostalgia, he experienced it here. The first gift of a Cannon camera from his father, the first photo contest he won at the university and the first assignment he ever accepted from a foreign press, all memorable moments of his life. Everything that ever counted for anything, he found it here. To leave these behind and start his life afresh in another land, even in the most disturbing period of times, would be like blasphemy to the sacred memories.

And then of course, there was MayLin. He wondered what she would say. It was easy for him to answer Sheryl, but when he pondered what MayLin's reply would be to the same question, he was not so sure if the explanation would be just as easy.

He kept these ruminations to himself and when he spoke, his words were vaguely misleading, almost to the point of being non sequitur.

"There's the house, of course. There's plenty of work to be done on it yet."

"Don't get obtuse with me, Jailudin. What house? That rundown heap of waste you call a house? You hardly lift a finger on the darn thing."

"I know, but I'll start on it as soon as I get a bit of time on my hand. You'll see, it'll be a beautiful house with colorful bay windows letting in plenty of sunlight."

They rambled on, freely and naturally as if picking up on shreds of conversations left unfinished when he was hastily whisked away. She was seated on a rattan chair by the bedside and he was reclining on the headboard, two dissimilar people from such vastly different cultural references, divergent paths converged and drawn amicably closer through the course of events.

The flow of their conversation was like a game of

shuttlecock. Each was determined in their goal to goad the other, shifting and shimmying, their awkward maneuvers were like a ritualistic dance that went on without end.

"You can always survive out there, you know. Your talent will be so much more appreciated. And there's a chance it'll flourish well under more auspicious circumstances."

"One day," he muttered. "Perhaps, one day."

The disbanded group reassembled a few hours later. If the unexpected siege by the police squad had given them immeasurable fright, they certainly did not show any sign of it on their faces. They had followed the same procedure that they had rehearsed tirelessly before each assignment. Should anything happen and the group had to disperse, they would reconvene again in a safe house whose exact location was made known only moments before the group rolled out to their next assignment. Now, back amongst themselves, they flitted about, bantering and kidding each other about the close shave.

"Phooooey, that was close," the leader drew a sigh of relief, and then quickly changed his tone, sounding all seriousness. "That taught us a lesson to be extra careful in our next assignment. We've got to make some significant changes. It seems that our jobs have turned into a pattern, too easy a pattern to be divined by these people. We'll have to alter our way of aiding our friends. We can't afford to allow this to happen to us again."

"I'll take a roll call, those of you that are still interested to stick around for the next assignment, do please let me know. Now, let's pray for a moment."

Immediately a rapt silence enwrapped the volunteers as they prayed, each in his faith, camaraderie of love bound by bountiful passion for charity. They had been chased away from their labor of love and their lives threatened, but fearlessly they had rebounded, and once more sticking out their necks.

The leader shed a tear, it was not a maudlin testament to their altruistic struggle but it was a tear of joy of knowledge. The knowledge that he was equal among peers, he felt his soul entwine and become one with the selfless determination of these volunteers.

A few days later, picking up one of the local papers, Jailudin read on the front page the banner headline spread out in bold type: "Nocturnal Charity Work Linked to Communists." After months of letting the issue kicked about in public debates, the Defense Minister had finally decided to put an end to the widespread speculation. He came out reluctantly to make an announcement. He vouched that after spending considerable time studying extensively the modus operandi of the Midnight

Charity Prowlers, the Ministry of Defense had concluded that there was strong evidence of a striking resemblance between MCP's movement to the working pattern of the communists. Details of the similarity were carefully laid out and compiled into lists made available to the journalists. Communists prowled stealthily in the cover of the night along mountainous terrain and so did the Midnight Charity Prowlers. Communists practiced community sharing which was not unlike that of Midnight Charity Prowlers. The list went on and on.

The ludicrous simplicity of the explanation made Jailudin laugh. It was as if by rearing the monstrous head of the ogre by the name of communism, everything would be solved. People would be appeased. Life went back to normal. For the last thirty years, this had been the acceptable explanation for everything, from mysterious bombings to the insurgency in Aceh, the special regent in Sumatra. Nothing much had changed.

With deft assistance from Sheryl, the damaged tendons on his toes began the slow process of healing. Now he was able to move a little around her apartment, making phone calls to keep up with things outside, hobbling to the kitchen for a cup of tea. Sheryl kept a watchful eye on him all the time, carefully seeing to his needs, yet discreet in her assistance. She took pains to make sure her helping hands did not appear too intrusive, or attract too much attention.

Jailudin was grateful for everything she did for him, but feared that he had overstayed her welcome. He could not wait to get back to the little room at his sister's house, back to the musty mess among his photography equipment and books, the cozy corner he called home.

Sometimes, when his sister, Fatima, visited him, one look at the disapproving expression on her face was enough to make Jailudin want to plead for her to drive him home. But he knew Sheryl would have none of that. In her quiet, determined way, she seemed to have taken charge of his total recovery program. Nothing was going to deter her in her single-minded purpose, not even Jailudin.

One balmy afternoon, Fatima came to see him. She carried with her a basket filled with all Jailudin's favorite delights: a variety of mouthwatering cakes from the market: coconut mousse, rice flour layered with fruits, the sweet doughy variety sprinkled with shreds of coconut or laced with a layer of Javanese brown sugar. He picked a sampling and placed it on the tip of his tongue, savoring it. A heavenly treat for his starved taste buds. He was helping himself on them with the ravishing hunger of a country boy when he noticed that Fatima was shuddering with tears.

He stopped, asking disconcertingly, "Something's the matter, Fatima?"

"It's Rizal," she wiped her nose nosily. "He hasn't been

home for a while."

"But where has he been?"

"He's in the mosque most of the time with his mob of friends."

"Well, why didn't you go and fetch him home?"

"He's changed, J!" she said, rendered even more disconsolate by the reality of her own words.

"How changed can he be? He's still your husband, father of your child. I know him; he's a good man, Fatma. You can't lose heart so easily."

Jailudin's words broke down the shaky defense, unleashing a rush of emotions tucked away for so long in a private corner of her impassive heart. She cried heartily.

"Take me to him," Jailudin leant on the arm of the sofa in the sitting room, struggling to his feet. "I'm sure I can talk some sense into him and ask him to go home."

"I don't know, J! I don't think he'd like that. In fact, I don't think he'd like that I'd come to you. J, he's completely changed. He's become..." she was too choked up with emotions to finish her sentence. Jailudin waited, patiently listening. His face was expressionless. He knew he should let her vent her anguish. It would be futile for him to rush her; it would only make things more complicated than it already was. But there were so many things he wanted to ask her. What had actually happened? Was there a row? What was it all about? The questions kept cropping up. They were driving him crazy.

He limped forward and for the first time in so many years he held her close to him in his arms. "Don't you worry. It will be all right."

"He's changed, J. He's like a man possessed."

Just then, Sheryl entered the apartment with two plastic bags overflowing with grocery. Shyly, Fatima extricated herself and sank back into the sofa, quietly wiping away the tears from her face. Sheryl looked inquiringly at Jailudin, but received only a baffled look from him.

Jailudin dragged his foot into the bedroom. When he reappeared a moment later, he looked sharp in his pressed shirt and pants.

"Let's go and fetch him," he said, holding Fatima's arm.

8

*I*t was after Dzuhur, the noon prayer. The small room at the top of the mosque was filled with the clinging smoke of clove cigarettes. It was thronged with men clad in flowing white robes over checkered sarongs, packing deep into the corner. From down below came intermittently the mellifluous chants of a group of children reciting from the Qur'an under the stern tutelage of a cleric.

It was an atmosphere of charged emotions. The men were talking rapidly at the same time, their faces contorted in the throes of arguments, flushed by the sweltering heat seeping down through the corrugated tin roofs above them.

"I know we're all passionate about the subject," Rizal counseled, trying to keep the session moving in orderly fashion. "But we shouldn't allow this to cause a rift among us. This is not the reason why we're here. This is supposed to be a friendly dialogue, so go easy."

The day's session was drifting dangerously to the brink of a major shouting match between the regulars. For some time now, the subject was vehemently tossed back and forth in the Octagonal Room: why should they continue their support of People's United Party, the party of choice for most pious Muslims?

"We can't abandon them just like that! After all, they've done a lot for our community. They've built mosques and helped eradicate illiteracy in the rural areas, and created opportunities for our economically weak brothers," a chubby, mustachioed middle-aged man yelled from the back row. "We must consider the consequences of our decision."

"What consequences? What have they achieved to justify our continuous support? Look at the children running bare feet at street junctions, panhandling, when they should be in class, learning survival skills. Panhandling, you call that an achievement?" a man with a stentorian voice challenged. "And nothing will be achieved unless we make drastic changes now. The party has become staidly bureaucratic, self-centered beyond belief and irrelevantly removed from the wishes and needs of the people. The leaders have become bloated, concerned only of keeping their asses in place. They're too busy with their lives to think of the little guys!"

A few men shouted their approval while others in the opposing camp hissed. A burst of sporadic noises swept the room as the men grappled hard with the thrust of the subject.

"Start a new party," someone hollered. "Call it PBI, Party of the Brotherly Islam!" There were grunts of almost unanimous agreement around the room and for a moment they seemed seized by the fervor of the idea, suddenly unified in their vision.

It was never meant to be anything but a casual gathering, a haphazard powwow session attended mostly by a straggly group of worshippers after the Friday prayer. It must have been the spontaneous nature of these sessions or the openly eclectic and electrifying atmosphere that made them so appealing to a steady stream of crowd now visiting the Octagonal Room daily. Some hailed from as far away as the community beyond the neighborhood.

In a short period of time, the rambling sessions began to be widely known as the Prayer Dialogue. While the format remained loose and almost rules-free, the handful of original members of the gathering soon took over. It became organized. With organization, there was an elected body of caretakers and with caretakers, there was a leader and with the leader, the manifesto of intents, thus the beginning of a political machine.

Rizal was the elected head of the boisterous group. He had accepted the leadership role bestowed upon him with the zeal of a chosen man. Night after night he stayed over in the small room, sleeping on the makeshift bed cursorily put together from planks assembled from the courtyard of the mosque. He was reading voraciously political and religious tracts, consumed entirely by the responsibility of the role of his newly chosen preoccupation. Any other matters outside of this were merely distractions, annoyances to be shunned, including among others, the tearful pleas from Fatima for him to return home.

"We must seriously think about the possibility," Rizal seized the moment. He had waited impatiently for someone to reach the inevitable subject of the new party so that he could intercede and legitimize the suggestion.

"We need a party for the little people. The impoverished men and women overlooked by the previous government, trampled by the irresponsibly rich, left to rot in the slums, unprotected by healthcare and security," he continued, his thoughts flowing with the smoothness of premeditated conviction.

"It will be a party that creates jobs for the poor and the needy," his voice soared, hovering with authority in the stuffy air above the rapt listeners. "It will be a party that provides first class education for the people, creating generations of learned and capable people, who will grow independent, free from reliance on the handouts from the rich. Most of all, it will be the party for the Muslims, guided by the unvarying teachings of Prophet Mohammed." Murmurs of approval rippled through the Octagonal Room.

"The moment is now. We must seize the momentum and make this a reality!"

"But how do we finance the party?" a man shouted, breaking the almost dreamlike rapture in the room and was readily shushed to silence for being so audacious as to interrupt the inspiring speech that was promising a vision of the utopian world.

Rizal responded to the man without missing a beat, "Why, that shouldn't present too much of a problem! Take it to the people. Talk to them, persuade them. If we make sense, I'm sure they'll listen. And when they listen, they will support us!"

"So why don't we stick to the present party and try to fix it so that it'll work toward our goals?"

"We can't. Because the People's United Party is changed. It is no longer the party that we're familiar with since our childhood. It's grown different. It is now the party for the middle class. Their politics are the politics of the middle class. Ours is the party of bus drivers, owners of *becaks*, storekeepers, gas station attendants, peasants, farmers, office boys, water vendors, receptionists, millions and millions more. These were the invisible people, insignificant statistics to most but they make up for over sixty percents of the entire population of this nation. They are the genuine population that we should be fighting for!"

By now, the gathering was charged. Rizal's words were like the ringing chimes that awakened their mordant sense of civic duty. They kept nodding their heads, endlessly muttering their approval as Rizal went on to bombard them with more facts, more truisms, more no-nonsense pictures of reality that all along they had been vaguely aware of but never paid too much attention to.

"Let's not wait for another day. Let's start our dream today," he said in the end. The pouch was passed around the room to begin the collection proceeding.

When the gathering slowly dispersed through the door, two men approached Rizal by the wooden round table in the middle of the room where he had stood making his flowing delivery. He was crowded around by a close group of his men, continuing the debates on the issues raised so heatedly only moments ago. The strangers' rather unusual appearance caught their attention.

They were striking in the white flowing tunic, one wizened old man and another in his late thirties, their heads wrapped snugly in elaborate white turbans. They appeared unruffled by the oppressive heat, standing upright and brisk in their regalia. They squinted at them from behind those rugged masks of inscrutable impassivity, from the flowing mass of wildly grown sideburns, moustaches and beards. The only light that came out of the fixed expression was the glint from their eyes.

"That was a rousing speech," the elderly man, who seemed to be the leader, cracked into a smile. He spoke a smattering of heavily accented *bahasa*, made worse by his lisping Arabic overtone.

"Thank you," Rizal said, straining hard to decipher the old man's rather elliptical *bahasa.* "You look unfamiliar to me. Have I seen you here before?"

"Oh, no, let me introduce myself. My name is Mustafa and this here is my associate, Maruf. We're here to help you achieve your dream."

Maruf, the quiet one with a vigilant expression on his face, watched impassively as Mustafa went on to explain to everyone the purpose of their visit. They had been sent by a progressive organization, whose identity, he said, must remain strictly in anonymity for the guardians did not wish to attract unnecessary attention for their philanthropy. He went on in his rasping, hoarse voice that their organization was established to advance the cause of Muslim worldwide and that it received generous endowments from a group of philanthropists in the Middle East.

"We've monitored your little organization for a while. We think it meets the criteria for application of aid from us."

The unexpected announcement exhilarated Rizal's men and kept them ticklish on their toes, wondering what other surprises would be forthcoming from these strangers. They pricked up their ears, listening attentively.

"There's only one thing," Mustafa paused. Rizal's men leant forward, waiting in heightened suspense. He continued, "Of course, you need to register your organization officially either here or internationally so that we can process your application."

When prodded by one of the followers about how big a sum the entitlement was, in his lilting voice, Mustafa said, "A quarter of a million dollars."

The men were agape. They were shocked by the generosity of the endowment, completely unprepared by the blessed good fortune of this spectacular proportion. Rizal made a quick conversion of the currency. It came close to about 2.5 billion rupiah in the current escalating exchange rate!

Having passed the news, Mustafa placed an application form on the wooden round table. And unceremoniously he said, "We shall be in touch!"

He took a keen look around the room and made a parting remark, "I think the place can use a bit of fixing up, don't you?"

As mysterious in the way of their appearance, in their departure they left a shroud of bafflement trailing behind them.

Rizal's men were beside themselves with joy. They had bottled up the urge to scream all the while the strangers were there, but as soon as they left the Octagonal Room they let out shrieks of incredulity.

"Oh, my God, this is absolutely unbelievable!" Ary, the loudest in the group, yelled in disbelief.

"Allah has spoken," Rizal said solemnly.

Since the appearance of the turbaned men from Middle East, things happened rapidly at the Octagonal Room. There was the sudden appearance of a batch of computers. The man from the delivery service simply asked Rizal to sign some papers and then delivered to him five brand-new Compaq computers, built in complete with CD–ROMs and modems. Service men materialized mysteriously and proceded to fix the rooftops, put fresh paints on the peeling, cracked walls and even put up two new air conditioners. Soon, cash checks worth large amount of money turned up in the donation pouch. It was an amazing time, but Rizal and his men took it all in good strides. "Allah has spoken," Rizal kept muttering.

Along with the frenetic pace of changes taking place in the Octagonal Room, Rizal noticed that there were also a number of unfamiliar faces cropping up in the regular sessions. They seemed to blend in awkwardly among the regular crowd.

They gathered mostly among themselves by the entrance, puffing at their cigarettes, showing not the least interest in what transpired inside.

Rizal was wary of these men. He watched them come and go. But because they did not interfere with the sessions and seemed to be on good terms with everyone in the gathering he left them alone and continued on the demanding tasks at hand. The sessions were no longer semantic debates on idealism, but had now developed into serious discourses on how to build more membership for the organization, setting up branch offices in key parts of Jakarta, and then branching out throughout Java.

With the question of money now conveniently out of the way, the plans became ambitious, bolder in vision and more expansive in scope.

Rizal was deeply steeped in one of these sessions with a handful of his close associates when he looked up and saw Jailudin at the door. He immediately asked for a few moments of privacy from his men.

"Come in, Jailudin," Rizal asked awkwardly.

Jailudin stepped onto the parquet floor, surveying the Octagonal Room, stacked up with boxes of books. There were clothes strewn haphazardly on the chairs by the window, on the sofa, strung on a string by the corner. It was a disorderly sight; Jailudin was dismayed by what he saw. He pulled up a chair and sat down in the middle of the room. He had not come for a confrontation, but somehow the bewildering mess he witnessed before his eyes unnerved him, giving him a disturbingly unpleasant sensation.

"What's going on, Rizal?" Jailudin said, wasting no time to cut straight to the heart of the matter.

"Well, as you can see, everything," he floundered, nervously extending his arms around him. "Everything's happening, Jailudin. For once, I feel like I'm doing something worthy for our religion and for our country."

"How about your family, Rizal!" Jailudin's voice was stern and intentionally emphatic. He felt it unforgivable that a man could cause such immeasurable pain to his beloved one. And it angered him even more by the thought that that beloved person was his sister.

"What about them, J?"

"What are you doing for them?"

There was a lengthened pause as Rizal's brows creased deeply into his forehead. After a while, he said, "I need some time for myself, J. I need to concentrate on this. The people need me." He looked appealingly round the empty room as if it was filled with supplicating faces beseeching his help.

"Your *family* needs you, Rizal. Don't you see how saddened and distraught they are right now? How can you go on with whatever crusade you've embarked on and forget that there are those beloved to you waiting for your return daily."

"It's not a crusade, J." There was a flash of anger in his eyes, but quickly as if stricken by remorse from Jailudin's words, it passed. He carried on in suppressed annoyance. "We're in the middle of building a party. It's a party for the little people."

"It sounds dangerous to me, Rizal. Politics by any other name is a dangerous thing. You're playing with fire. I hope you know what you're doing," Jailudin stared firmly into his eyes. "I'm here not in the capacity of a private counsel to your personal affairs. I'm here for my sister, who seems terribly miserable right now."

"I really couldn't care less what you plan to do with your party or whatever crazy idea that will seize you in the future, but do please tread carefully, because every step you take, you carry three other human lives with you, your wife and two children."

The harsh words struck him hard. He was beaten down, smarting with pain. Jailudin was unrelenting; he was not about to call it quits so easily. He continued, "I know, I cannot ask you to do as I wish, but at least consider what they would like you to do now!"

Having said that he rose from his chair. He cast one quick scathing look at Rizal, whose head was stooped down laden with remorse and limped toward the door.

Outside, Fatima stood by the railing near the fence, waiting anxiously. As soon as she saw him emerge from the gate of the mosque, she moved hurriedly toward him. She held on to his hand, helping him along the gravel path.

"How's he, J!"

"He's crazed, Fatima. Those idling days of unemployment, sitting on his own at home and at the mosque must have gotten to his head, eaten away all his good senses. He's now striving to be a politician. Imagine that!" Jailudin shook his head in bafflement.

"Is he coming home, J?"

"I'm not sure. Maybe we should just let him be for a while, let him air out all those excessive emotions. Then, maybe when he's good and ready, he'll come home," he held her hand close to him, feeling deeply for her anguish.

With time, the Octagonal Room bloated with overflowing effects. On top of the boxes of Rizal's books were now piled haphazardly with samples of banners painted with the new party's emblem and pamphlets everywhere. It was so packed with things it had to expand. Which it slowly did, first by pulling down the wall, then pushing outward into the empty spaces outside the window toward the parapet.

Rizal was beginning to get used to the sight of strangers

flitting in and out, scruffy, mean looking men with dark curly hair wearing short sleeved shirts, their shirt ends rolled up showing off well-honed biceps. He never quite understood what they were looking to gain from loitering in the premises.

As the members grew, it had become more and more difficult for Rizal and his men to regulate attendance and keep track of everyone. To encourage an openly engaging atmosphere there was never any specific rule of conduct in the Octagonal Room. Any stranger could freely wander into the room and went for the wooden round table in the center and promulgated just about any crazed idea that took his fancy that day. Of course they also took a risk of being booed.

One quiet day, a man staggered to the wooden table and seized the floor. He was one of the men wearing the short-sleeved shirt. He stood wobbly, looking as if he was going to collapse at any moment. He warbled incomprehensibly. When the men clamored for him to speak louder, he held up his hand to keep silence, and then continued mumbling away. In his floundering, fumbling way, he seemed to be saying the same words over and over. When the men started booing him he raised his voice, venomously chanting, "Banish the Christians. Kick out the Chinese. Reclaim our religion, take back our country!"

There was a sporadic applause from a cluster of men, who goaded the drunken man along, amused by the unexpected diversion but the room soon lapsed into silence. Then, a shout rose up from a corner, "Let's take down the church, chase the Chinese out of town!" The Octagonal Room was flung into a roiling atmosphere resounding with voices of disparate, vociferous views. The shouting bouts had gotten to such a maddening racket that it was no longer possible to hear what everyone was saying.

"Let's all keep calm," Rizal shouted, the moment he dreaded most seemed to be happening before him. He was staring straight into the blazing red eyes of hate. "We've set up these sessions so that we will talk and behave sensibly, not bouncing around like a bunch of savages!"

"Stop the flowery speech, burn their shops, burn their cars, burn their houses!" the voice in the corner egged on, persistent in his provocation. "Take action, now!"

Days of such psychedelic turns that switched abruptly in mood swings, from passionate discussions of lifting the poor and the helpless out of their plights, hurtling inexplicably into the provocative subjects of racism and religion, became quite common occurrences at the Octagonal Room. The incendiary topics sidetracked the gathering into workout sessions of hatred and extreme racism, keeping them off issues of great importance that required urgent attention. Rizal was appalled. He had a gnawing fear that he had lost control of the sessions. He wondered if troublemakers might have usurped the

Octagonal Room, and were now sowing seeds of hatred.

After one of these tirades that seemed to drone on irritatingly, Rizal and his men stormed out of the Octagonal Room in disgust. They made their way through the alley to their regular stop at Udin's *waroeng*, a simple tented food stall, behind the mosque. All through the way there, they were searching for ways to curb the unwarranted outbursts that had so annoyingly disrupted their work at the Octagonal Room.

They had hardly arrived for a short while when a fistfight broke out between one of Rizal's men and a small scruffy-looking man. It was a simple case of misunderstanding, which, in ordinary circumstances, could have been resolved easily without causing any hard feelings. Rizal's man must have taken the other man's order of steamed noodles by mistake and unwittingly slurped down the food, rendering the man bilious with rage. A simple word of apology would have sufficed to remedy the situation and end it with an affable handshake, yet the small, scruffy man was adamant, dead set on picking a fight. When profuse apology from Rizal's man was summarily turned down, fisticuffs were soon traded. Before long the two men were going after each other's neck, wrestling for their lives on the ground. They were at first cheered rowdily from the side by a group of supporters. As the fracas became more feverish, they too jumped into the fray, hurling rocks and shouting invectives at each other. It was a total bedlam. Rizal watched with growing horror at the raw emotional charge that was spreading widely and with such electrifying intensity.

The police were called in to disperse the scuffle. What started out as a tussle between two men, through the grapevine, became a fractious conflict of such religious proportions. Words quickly got out that the Muslims were beating up the Christians, or through a different channel, the truth was reversed. Rumors spread rapidly like a contagious disease, and soon after the police left, cuffing the men embroiled in the fight, a busload of hissing and fuming men came back, armed fully with lead pipes, crowbars and knives. Unable to get Rizal's men, they unleashed their fury at Udin's stall, setting it in flames. The fire flared up in the crackling dry air, spreading up and up the walls, flapping and roaring through the windows before blazing into the mosque.

Within a few hours, the mosque was consumed in flames. The whole neighborhood was stirring; the residents were shaken by the swiftness of the event. Stricken by fear of yet another pogrom, they started to leave their houses in droves. The streets were clogged with cars jostling and wrangling to make a clean break.

Rizal watched the mosque slowly swallowed by the engulfing flames. All the efforts he had put in it for the last few months now evaporated into a cloud of smoke. He stood in the shade of a tree, gazing fixedly at what used to be home to his soul, refuge to his newfound purpose in life, now steadily reduced to cinders, to bitterness, to nothingness.

There was anger welling up inside him. He felt betrayed. He felt strongly that he had been used like a marionette by some invisible force to wreak havoc and disharmony. The realization pained him and filled him with insufferable disgust.

9

*T*he night before the charity event, Jailudin ran into MayLin. They froze on their tracks at an intersection of the sprawling Jakarta Festival Fair Ground, the site of the night of charity. The air was filled with the stammering din from the site where workmen were rigging up the scaffoldings to build the lofty main stage. Vendors of various kinds vied with one and the other by flaunting their goods: from handicrafts, kites, and wooden miniatures to appetizing offerings of local delights. The stands were aligned on both sides of the lane leading up to the main event area in the center.

MayLin seemed startled by the chance encounter. There was a moment of awkwardness as they stood silently in the center of the whirling madness: she was holding a brownbag tightly in her arms, florid and breathless in the uncertain light from the fair ground lamps, and Jailudin was smiling blandly.

"I heard what happened to you," she finally broke the silence, in spurts of uneasy glibness. "Thank you for kindly warning us. We know all along they're up to something." Inadvertently she looked around her, watching out for the phantoms that seemed to hound her wherever she went. It was a compulsive behavior that had lately grown to become an involuntary habit. Then, she continued breathlessly, "It's really unforgivable what they've done to you! Absolutely shameless!"

Jailudin shrugged, watching with keen interest how her face shifted in the lights and became so lively animated when she talked. He reveled in the fluid, rushing freedom of his unclogged breathing.

"Are you avoiding me, MayLin?" The words tripped out of his mouth just like that, abruptly, bluntly, and totally incongruous to the occasion. The audacity of it took him by surprise, held him in nervous trepidation while he watched her mien change gradually.

"I didn't mean it to be that way," she said, eyes fixedly staring at the concrete pavement beneath her feet.

Encouraged, Jailudin pursued, "Then, why?"

"I've been busy," she said succinctly.

"Well, so busy you couldn't even say hello?"

She propped up her head, for the first time, looking levelly into his eyes. "I'm so sorry, I didn't get the chance to see you when you were laid up at Sheryl's."

"It's all right. I thought you might come up with some interesting excuse when we meet. Anything would have been more intriguing than the tiresome refrain: 'I've been busy!' Thought I heard that one somewhere before."

She laughed and her face turned florid with abashment. Jailudin gasped at the incomparable beauty unfolding in such proximity to him. Inebriated, steeped in the heady freedom of his olfactory system, he felt as if he could breathe her in, swallowing whole the transcending beauty, making it forever a part of him.

"You're not ever going to let me slip out of this one, are you?" she asked.

"Not if I can help it, no!" Jailudin insisted.

She sidled over to a bench by the lamppost and sat down, letting the brownbag containing some décor items for the stage drop to the ground. Jailudin slumped down on the other end of the bench.

The fair ground loomed before them, shrouded in the silhouette of dusk's failing light, a sprawling vista of stony facades of deserted shops and kiosks. He could not have conjured up a more idyllic place to meet and talk with her.

"Look what you've done?" she said, smiling in the light-hearted, engaging way that he had seen her often do in so many occasions.

"What have I done to you?"

"You're making me procrastinate," she said, with a feigned reprimanding tone.

"Maybe you deserve a little of that," he said, incredulous that they were carrying on so well. "You seem to be always fighting for something, for the reformist students, for the victims of rape, for the poor…what about yourself, what do you fight for yourself?"

There was a brooding silence. A dark, downcast look came over her face. She sulked visibly, absorbed in the depths of her own thoughts. "Nothing," she said afterward, tersely with a surprising finality that caused Jailudin to look up at her. "Nothing of consequence," she muttered, then the tone in her voice changed, she asked mischievously, "And you J, what would you fight for?"

"You," Jailudin said, shocked by the temerity of his admission.

"Excuse me?" she asked, mortified by the directness of Jailudin's reply.

"I won't fight for any fight in the world," he said, with such eloquence that it surprised even himself. "I won't fight for the freedom of the press. I won't fight for the eradication of poverty from mankind," the words tumbled out of his mouth. He had to pause to catch his breath. "I won't fight for the betterment of the environment, the forests, the animal habitats, but..." he paused, his voice quavering with tenderness. "...but I will fight for you."

She was completely blown away by the droll, roll call display of emotions.

"Jailudin, you're absolutely, preposterously, certifiably mad!" she shrieked, hysterical with laughter.

"You, my lady, will be worth a fight," Jailudin said with unwavering seriousness.

"It's truly very cavalier of you. I'm eternally grateful!" she said and made a curtsey. She then leant over to give him a peck on his forehead.

"I never had this urge to fight for anything in my life," Jailudin continued, his solemn tenacity kept MayLin from bursting out with giggles. "All my life, I've been in this tortoise shell, sheltered, peering at the world from a safe distance. But now, everything's changed. Now, I know what's worth fighting for!"

MayLin appeared uncomfortable for a moment by his persistence. Then softly she murmured, "You won't win."

"But why ever not? Anyway, it'll still be worth a fight," Jailudin said, his voice growing shrill with determination.

"Such paths have been trudged through before, J! They lead to misery and pain."

"It's still worth a fight."

MayLin was all too familiar with scenes of such a union. She had oftentimes witnessed how the mixed couple, usually the *other* spouse, who would be tactfully tackled or simply overlooked in family gatherings. Everyone seemed eager to comport himself with a certain flair of indifference, sporting a bit of savoir-faire by showing no raised eyebrows. But the furtive glances, the hushed whispers, the overly kind gestures gave the game away, displaying in abundance the unspoken fear of *otherness* in the other person.

"You won't win," she said, unconsciously biting her thumbnail. "It's not going to be a fair fight."

"It's not about winning," he persisted, picking up enough courage to slide over the bench to her and grasped her hand. "It's the journey on the way to winning that counts!"

MayLin gave him a wan smile and they kissed ferociously right there in the bench, as if they were shuttered away from the spinning world, locked in the safe haven of their beating, thumping hearts.

MayLin gently pulled away. "Now, you know why I have been avoiding you!" she said enigmatically. She picked up the brownbag and rose hastily. "Trust me, it wouldn't be a good fight." With that she walked away, her shoes clacking away on the concrete pavement, trailing shreds of Jailudin in her wake.

Jailudin was wrapped in the dizzying haze of love. The world was irrelevant. The ceaseless racket from the construction workers was muffled by the roiling emotions inside him.

It was the heavenly kiss that ultimately set him free, and yet now it would keep him forever imprisoned in the reservoirs of its painful memory. How could beauty so effortless be possible!

He was perplexed by her melancholic resignation. What could she have meant when she said he could not win? Who would stand in their way? Surely anyone who had ever experienced beauty of this magnitude, such uplifting radiance of the soul, could find it in his heart to refuse their love! Love was a divine blessing, a precious safe keeping on loan from heavenly provenance. How could she give it all up so easily?

When he opened his eyes, he lost her again for the second times. There was not a single thing in the world that could fill in the void left by her. The scenery that spanned before him with such splendor moments ago now lost its luster, a jumble of disarray in disconsolate incomprehension. He felt a pang widening inside him as he slouched spiritlessly toward a souvenir stand where he had left Sheryl engrossed in some handicrafts.

MayLin held her head, dragging her feet that were growing leaden with grief. She knew she had to be cold-hearted and killed it there and then, not taking the slightest chance of letting it flourish and bloom into what would eventually be inevitable gloom. As soon as she was out of his sight, she took off her shoes and ran. Tears streaked down her face, tearing her apart. She dashed around the scaffoldings of the main stage toward the makeshift tent built for the organizers.

When she saw Rafida, she collapsed into her arms, bawling out to her heart's content. Unprepared for the sudden outpouring, yet affected profoundly by the shudders of her grief, she could not help but cry along with her. Quizzically, the group of volunteers watched the two women locked in the embrace of each other's arms, howling wretchedly. It was not an unusual sight for the volunteers to witness tears being shed, for after all grief was what they dealt with on a daily basis, but this was different. These were their leaders, two of the staunchest and most strong-willed women they had ever known, and to see them wrecked by so much pain, it made them weep.

They came over to the inconsolably aggrieved women. In stuttering, tear-jerking voices, they tried to comfort them. The elderly in the group took the lead in dispensing their consolation. Unsure of what exactly prompted the grief, they generalized in their approach, calling upon the well-plied words of commiseration, invoking the wisdom of patience, tolerance and submission. Everything came to a halt. The makeshift tent pulsated with convulsions of unfathomable grief.

All through the way back, Jailudin sat by Sheryl's side, muted, heavy with the tremendous burden of agony. His world had opened up for a moment with magical wonderment, bristling with the prospect of hope, and then without warning it was shuttered, leaving him stranded in the depths of gloom. What he had glimpsed in that brief moment of enchantment would now be cherished like forbidden treasures. Every shade of every color, the tiniest of gestures, words spoken or unspoken, would be kept locked away in the reservoir of his memory to be recalled at any moment into life again and again.

He tried to intellectualize what had happened, to keep things in orderly perspectives. Things of the heart confounded him tremendously. He would not know how to put certain things together. He never understood for instance why whenever the impetus for intimacy arose, instead of seizing it, she seemed to push him away, always trying to pluck herself out of the situation and fleeing desperately for her life.

He plumbed the depths of reason to find a satisfying answer. He tried to reason with himself, to argue himself out of the rotten rut that he had gotten himself into and which had so mercilessly ravaged his soul.

So like a tortoise after a full day's excursion in the sun-blessed beach, he recoiled back into the shelter of his shell, smarting from the rigors of blistering weather.

"Are you all right, J?" Sheryl's voice resounded through

a long tunnel of reverie and transported him back to reality.

"Yes, I'm fine. It must be the darn humidity."

He was not aware of how long they had been standing there by his side. But when he turned his head, he saw them, the colorful turbans and the long flowing white tunic trailing in the wind. It was the men from Middle East. They seemed to have a way of popping up at the strangest juncture, like ominous bearers of tidings.

"Do not despair," said Mustafa, the stately elderly man. Then, in hymnal solemnity, he started to recite, "*...But when the sight is dazed and the moon is eclipsed, and the sun and moon are brought together, upon that day man shall say, 'Whither to flee?' No indeed; not a refuge! Upon that day man shall be told his former deeds and his nay, man shall be a clear proof against himself, even though he offer his excuses.*"

The verses, which Rizal recognized were quoted from the Chapter of Resurrection from the Qur'an, were delivered mellifluously in rhythmic Arabic.

"Who are you people?" Rizal stood aside, eyes ablaze with burgeoning anger. "Look at how much destruction you've caused!"

"We're your friends," Mustafa said calmly, not in the least ruffled by Rizal's accusatory remarks. "Come with us.

Maybe what we'll show you will bring a smile on your face."

His tone was suave, even mildly encouraging, yet the way he shoved him along, left no room for second guessing about his clear intent. They showed him the way to a white Volkswagen caravan parked on the edge of the road. It took them a while to wrestle out of the congested streets, then whisking briskly away onto the toll road, heading toward the seclusion of the hills in Puncak.

They stopped outside a gate that led through a meandering path overshadowed by a clump of tall, overarching trees, then emerging into an expansive clearing overlooking a breathtaking landscape of swooping, verdant hills. It was easily a few hundred hectares of sprawling land overgrown with tall swaying brushes, with sporadic tufts of wildflowers dotting the fields. Mustafa stepped down gingerly from the caravan. He strode ahead of them in a brisk, steady step, his long white robe trailing behind him, fluttering in the blustery winds. He let himself in through the gate and stood half submerged in the tall shrubbery, motionless, heedlessly encapsulated in the reflective serenity of the wide expanse.

"This will be our new home," he said, flailing both his arms to embrace the vast expanse. "It will be the ministry of our faith. It will be our fort against the transgressors. We'll train young men to fight for our cause, just like our forefathers before us, fighting for centuries on our behalf. And you…you shall be their elected leader, leading them to the path of righteousness." His eyes flickered with the manic intensity of a very determined man.

Rizal watched with the shocked miscomprehension of a man barely rising from the shards of a nightmare. It was a swift transition from crashing despair to this, the almost magical promise of hope.

"Come this way," Mustafa waved at him, heaving through the bracken overgrowth to a shed, a dilapidated wooden structure left to ruin in the withering effects of the weather, forgotten by time.

Mustafa untied the chain lock. The door opened with a rusty creak, revealing a dusty interior, festooned with entwining threads of gossamer. He stood aside by the door, ushering them in. As they brushed past the cobwebs into the shed, motes of dust swirled up in the wake of their steps. There was nothing in the shed, except for a row of crates neatly stacked up to one side of the ramshackle wall.

From a leather pouch he produced from underneath his robe, he extricated a jangle of keys. He picked one out and fitted it perfectly into the lock on one of the crates. It clicked and snapped open. He pulled up the lid, unveiling in the uncertain mottled light a stockpile of weapons: grenades, rocket launchers and machine guns.

"Whatever are these for?" Rizal recoiled at the sight of

the menacing killing tools. Tangible and within an arm's length away, he saw his fear looming large before him in the form of bearded men from Middle East.

"These are the notorious AK-47," he paused, lifting a machine gun from inside the crate, cradling it like a child in his arm and aiming it at the empty spaces through the door. "Sometimes in our struggle for change, we'll encounter obstacles. But you see, obstacles must be taken down!" He fired the unloaded machine gun, triggering a series of metallic bursts, *tack, clack, tack*...the eerie metallic clicks made Rizal's skin crawl. His mind must have played tricks with his hearing, for he thought he heard actual explosions of gunfire emanating from the machine gun. He felt a chill creeping down his spine.

"You see, there can be no progress, unless we're willing to stake our body and soul for the cause! There's no compromise, remember that, Rizal!"

"I'll have no part in this," Rizal said, darting a quick, nervous glance to see if they took offence by his remark. There was not a glimmer of movement on the impassively rugged countenances. They showed no trace of emotions, except for a twitch or an occasional tic on their shoulders to suggest their minds' process.

"Oh, of course, of course," Mustafa said, his face an impassive mask set in a permanent scowl. "It's understandable. But you needn't worry about that, Maruf will take care of that," he pulled up his gun and point at the taciturn man, who made a quiet nod in acknowledgment.

Mustafa gingerly returned the machine gun into the crate, then lowered the lid back on and put the lock in place. He brushed the dust off his hands and motioned imperatively for Rizal to follow him.

Back in the brilliant sunlight, feeling the soft afternoon breeze in his face, Rizal stood by the edge of the sheer precipice, anxiously watching the men's every movement, wondering nervously what they might be thinking to do next. He shuddered to think what these men were capable of doing.

"Now, we shall turn a new page in the history of our people's struggle," Mustafa said, gazing distractedly into the distance. Rizal was perplexed by what he meant by *our people*. He was not sure whether he meant in general all the people of the faith or Rizal's people or he had some other mystifying notion.

They must have stood there for an hour or so when suddenly Rizal heard rumbling from the path they had driven through. Hooting and hydraulic air brakes hissing, the trucks emerged from the path in the woods, big and sleekly sinewy, screeching to a halt. Men clad in blue overalls, wearing yellow safety helmets, bounced out, and shortly after heavy equipment, forklifts, bulldozers and cranes, were one by one trundled down, and immediately manned to move slabs of cement blocks and wooden frames toward an area marked for construction.

An ear-splitting din rose in the midst of the picturesque expanse, shattering irreversibly the once unassailable calm.

"What on earth are they doing?" Rizal asked.

"They're building our dream!" Mustafa said mystically, twirling the long, curlicue ends of his beard. "Or more like the fortress of our dream!"

10

"*M*aybe we should eat out tonight, J!" Sheryl proposed. There was something in her invitation that sounded so comforting to Jailudin's ears. Maybe it was the familiarity in the tone of her voice or maybe it was just the gesture, the very idea of someone asking him to dinner. It sounded so natural; it made him feel in the cozy company of an intimate friend.

The reason she made the suggestion was, of course, because for the last week, they had been having dinner at Sheryl's. It had been a most intriguing week of dietary adventure for Jailudin. He had never in his life tasted such far-ranging dishes, from Mexican, Italian to Chinese cuisine, all within the same week, all served in such perfection as deserving the approval of a Maitre D'.

"Wonderful idea," Jailudin said. "Only if you allow me to buy dinner."

"That sounds even better," she said.

Jailudin suggested the Balinese restaurant in Kemang, South Jakarta. He had had a full week's introduction to the world's cuisine, now he craved the spicy, tasty Indonesian dish. Upon hearing the suggestion, Sheryl winced. Although she had taught herself well to survive the hazards of the roadside stalls, she had never grown accustomed to spicy cuisine. And she knew that the place they were going to served really tongue scorching stuff.

Half way through her seafood basket, a combination dish that included sticks of prawns, squid and fish complimented with fresh cauliflower leaves to be eaten with the chili and onion paste, she was drenched with perspiration.

"It tastes absolutely marvelous," she said cheekily, mopping her face with Kleenex after Kleenex, a cannonball of fire waiting to spew through her mouth, inflaming the entire table.

"I knew you would love this kind of food," Jailudin enjoyed the pitiful sight of Sheryl trying frantically to stanch the unceasing, copiously flowing perspiration. "This is the absolute best place for this sort of spicy food."

"Remind me next time to bring along a fire extinguisher," she pouted, displaying a miffed expression on her flushing countenance.

They bantered and poked fun at one another. They

were simply two grownups in a playful interval. He wondered why it was so easy with Sheryl. There was never any compunction about how they should behave, or excessive worry about whether people would look. Everything seemed natural, carefree, and so normal.

When the plates were all cleared, over a cup of coffee, Sheryl spoke softly, lifting a finger and pointing at his heart, "I knew there's plenty of pain in there, J!"

The lingering mischief on his face vanished. He fell silent instantly.

"I don't know what you're talking about," he froze over his cup of coffee.

"She told me, J! I knew everything."

He looked up at her, greatly bewildered.

"What did she tell you?" he asked. There was sudden panic in his voice.

"She was sundered, J!" she said. "She had to confide in someone, or she'd explode. She really cared for you!"

Jailudin was wordless, submerged in a quandary of embarrassment. The dinner had been wonderful, graced with just a perfect dose of light humor and wisecracks. He would have preferred to finish it on that same cheerful note. Sheryl, however, must have thought differently. Why did she have to mention her? The skeletons had tumbled out of the closet. Secrets, once out in the open, would be hard to contain. They suddenly had a will of their own, free agents, prancing, cavorting, and trampling recklessly all over sacred personal grounds.

He knew he would never be able to burrow his way out of this, and neither would Sheryl allow him to knuckle down and slow burn over it.

"How could you say that? How could you confuse quitting with caring?"

"She knew it better than anyone, J! She knew you would suffer tremendously in the long run. It would be too selfish of her if she allowed that to happen."

"That's beside the point. Whether it's going to work or not, she should at least give it a fair shake. That way, at least, I would not have to go through life wondering, 'What if?'"

"She knew, J. Better than you or anyone about how her family or more precisely the rest of her family would react to this kind of relationship. Most of all, she cared for you too much to allow hubris like this to hurt you. Believe me, J. She meant well."

"Don't say that," he scowled, infuriated that anybody should try to shield him from the vagaries of life. He knew exactly what it involved and was ready for whatever that was forthcoming. He could handle it. But what he could not handle was the fact that she could so easily relinquish something of such magnificence. It must have taken a heart as hard as a rock, cold as a block of ice, to be so much in control, to be incapable of love, immune to the beauty of the experience, and most of all to be capable of such a horrendous act. It puzzled him endlessly that MayLin could be such a person.

They had stayed on, after the cup of coffee they ordered some beer. Jailudin was loath to move. Sorrow, like gravity, was cumbrous. It had a way of pulling a person down, entrenched him in the quagmire of pain and anguish, and wracked by the torment of memory.

By the time they left the restaurant, it was almost two in the morning. They were light-headed, cheerful again, though not somberly so. They whistled and hummed little advertising ditties all the way to Sheryl's apartment. Traces of sadness evaporated in the haze of alcohol.

It was hard to tell later, whether it was liquor or frustrated passion that should have been blamed for what eventually happened. For unconsciously they wrapped their arms around each other, pressing their warm cheeks together, playfully tweaking their noses. The kiss came next, fast and furious, lashing out with the force of vengeance.

They peeled away each other's clothes, thrashing on the bed, frantic in their fumbling clumsiness. The rest was a blur. A blob of fuzzy details in a chain of events. There was not a moment salvaged in its entirety, nor a second regained in the fullest of its nostalgic significance.

When he awoke the next day, Sheryl was not in bed, which was a tremendous relief for him since he would not have known how he would react under the circumstances. Would he have exclaimed with a cheerful note, "What a lovely morning! How was your sleep, dear?" No, he was not capable of such an impossible feat. He knew he would invariably cringe.

She had apparently gone out on an errand he thought and remained impassively in bed, long after he was fully awake, wracking his mind to retrieve a single fragment from the emotional jigsaw puzzle of the night before. Memory had a funny way of denying one's access when it was most urgently needed. No matter how hard he tried he could not summon up anything of significance. It could easily have been a dream, fleeting and ephemerally elusive.

He heard the key in the door to the apartment and stealthily like a child who had been punished to stay in bed; he slid back into the sheets, shutting his eyes to feign sleep. Moments later, the sound of sandals shuffled closer to the bedside. And soon after he felt a wet, voluptuous kiss smacking on his forehead and a lithe finger stroking the side of his face. He opened his eyes and saw Sheryl's radiantly smiling face hovering over him. He realized it was not a dream.

All through the night, the men in yellow safety helmets pounded away, shifting slabs after slabs of cement blocks onto the construction site. They were back in the warmth of the caravan, reclining on their seats, watching the hubbub of frenzied activities through the gap in the open sliding door. As the hours drew near to morning, Mustafa, the bleary-eyed old man, became frantic, shouting instructions into his phone. Before the crack of dawn, the unshaped block of construction began to take on a form. It was shaping to become a huge edifice with minarets rising like the supplicating hands of worshippers toward the heavens.

"This," Mustafa pointed at the building slowly rising out of the whirling debris, "This would be the center of all our future operations!" There was not the slightest hint of expression on his face, but his voice betrayed a trace of pride and there was smoldering frenzy in his eyes.

"Now, let's get to work!" he said and got out of the caravan.

Rizal rubbed his eyes wearily. It had been a long night's vigil; his ears were rash from the wizened old man's prickly harangue. He had no idea how long they intended to keep him and what nasty surprises they had in store for him. Although his heart was beating wildly with trepidation, he nonetheless kept a calm exterior, keeping a steady, unfaltering step behind them. He knew that the only chance he had to get out of there was by keeping calm, quietly waiting for the right opportunity.

Rizal plodded along in silence, following the path shone by Mustafa's flashlight. He led them all the way to the top of a ridge and then stopped. Rizal strained his eye to make out the darkened shapes in the midst of the swaying field. He could discern that there were three Volkswagen caravans lurking in the darkness, whitely luminescent in the moonlight, with the engines cut, forming a semicircle. Mustafa switched off his flashlight. Almost in an instance, the headlights on the caravans were switched on, casting a bright powerful circle of illumination on a patch of swaying copse. Three men were flung down to their knees into the circle of light. Stripped naked, blindfolded with their hands tied in a knot behind their back, they writhed and shivered like leaves in the morning air. They must have kicked and revolted for hours in vain, because now they appeared submissive and lifeless, completely resigned to their fate.

"These are the very same men who caused the fire on the mosque," Mustafa's raspy voice filled the air with echoes of commanding authority. "These are the rabble rousers, spineless weaklings used by cunning politicians. These are the kind of worthless people who stain the reputation of our faith."

He stopped and gave Maruf a signal. Deftly, without a moment's hesitation, Maruf pulled out a revolver and shot the men successively in the head. The shots rang out in rapid spurts, resounding through the hills, lingering in the air long after the men fell down, one by one into the underbrush.

It struck him without warning, like a bolt of lightning on a sunny afternoon. The realization dawned on him belatedly only moments later. It hit him hard, squeezed all the breath out of him, making him gag. He cowered down, yelping like a frightened animal. He flailed his hand ceaselessly in a gesture to shake off the horror that kept coming back to him like a recurring nightmare, each time with a greater force of details, sharper, meaner and more devastatingly real. He felt nauseated, his hands moist from the viciously palpitating heart, beads of perspiration sleeked down from his temples.

He summoned all the remaining strength in his body and made himself rise. Then as if abruptly seized by a charge of electricity he hopped and heaved through the thick underbrush, fleeing pell-mell toward the opening in the woods.

11

*I*t was a perfect evening for fanfares and festivities. The air was brisk, moist and cool, with a tremor of light breeze. The moon was radiantly cascading aloft. Not even a cloud was visible to impinge on its brilliance.

The anticipated moment finally arrived. It had taken plenty of anxious hours of preparations, and days of endless perseverance. But the evening opened without any hint of fatigue, it moved with the effortless smoothness of a well-oiled cog, buzzing with tremors of excitement. The list of distinguished guests graced the red carpet sashaying their way to their seats by the main stage, blitzed by a barrage of journalists' cameras. They consisted of the preeminent figures in the Jakarta's cultural and intellectual circles. And as if intentionally meant to be a form of rebuke to the way they handled the rape cases, no government officials were invited.

The tickets were sold out within hours of sale. Now, scalpers prowled the entrance, hawking the few spare tickets. Even before the curtain was lifted for the night's event, there was a burgeoning sense of euphoria among the organizers that it was going to be a success.

It opened with the welcoming fanfares of *gamelan* music, followed seamlessly by the graceful choreography of *Legong,* the celestial Balinese ritual dance. And the night took off, enchanting the spectators, and at intervals taunting them with the sardonic wit of the city's best comedians. It was slowly building on its course toward the anticipated finale when the auction of antiques would be held. The antique collections had been solicited from prominent personalities from both business and artistic communities, among them MayLin's father, who was entirely unaware that his marble Venetian statue of a cherub had been conveniently borrowed for charity.

MayLin watched with satisfaction from behind the curtain, dressed in the elegantly tight-fitting silk Kebaya, her hair bundled up into a bun, the spitting image of the traditional matron.

She had dreamt of this moment for months. It was as if all her life she had worked toward the realization of this moment: standing by the curtain, witnessing the seeds of her hard labor take shape, touching so many people. She was seized by a sense of gratification, not for herself or for the efforts she put in the project, but for the people in her community. This was the night when she hoped the disparate worlds coincided for the higher calling of charity. People from diverse ethnic and cultural backgrounds finally united in their efforts to condemn any form of aggression on women. It was to mark as a model precedent for bigger and more ambitious projects to be carried out in the future by others in the Chinese community. It was to open their eyes to the possibilities of organized charity, an encouraging prelude to lure them out in the open, to take their rightful place, to engage in what mattered most to them and everyone else, and to have the courage to lead where they could contribute most.

But the evening would never be complete unless she could find the one person who counted most in all her travails. She searched in the teeming sea of spectators, but could not find him. She saw his works, instead. The black and white images culled from his photo essay on rape victims. The gaunt faces imprinted on banners, wavering melancholically on the poles. She was filled with an inexplicable feeling of depraved emptiness, as if all her labor had failed to accomplish the one thing that counted most to her: to have his presence in the most important evening of her life.

Crestfallen, she turned and walked down the steep wooden steps toward the makeshift tent. Inside, it was seething with frenzied bustle. In alternating frequency, the group of artists and dancers rushed in and out of the stuffy, narrow space strewn with props, costumes and sundry paraphernalia for the show. Rafida was engulfed in the midst of the madness, now crouching down to trim the hem of a costume, in another moment, transformed as the resident makeup specialist.

As she wove her way through the frantic knot of people to her little corner at the back of the partitioned changing room, she found him seated on the straight-backed chair by her desk, with a bouquet of flowers in his hand, waiting patiently, unaffected by the whirligig around him. Sheryl was leaning on the wall by his side, wearing a bemused expression on her face.

"Are these for me?" she said, looking at the flowers in Jailudin's hand.

"Oh, yes," Jailudin snapped out of his stupor. "Here, congratulations!"

"Well done," Sheryl said, coming over to hug and kiss her. "You've done a wonderful job, MayLin!"

She blushed, uncomfortable with the effusive compliments, but greatly pleased to see that he was there. Softly, almost inaudibly in the prevalent racket, she said, "Thanks, you've done so much for us!"

Then they lost the thread of conversation. MayLin fiddled with the petals of the rose bouquet while Jailudin stared intently at the costumes lying in a heap on the ground.

Imperceptibly, Sheryl withdrew from the room, retreating to a bench outside of the makeshift tent.

Out in the open, Sheryl breathed a sigh of relief. The air was stirring with the clamor of the milling crowd and punctuated by sudden bursts of laughter from the spectators. It was a night tinged with ebullience, yet she felt terribly wretched. She could see it in those droopy, dark eyes that he was not going to get over her. She told herself not to be affected by shenanigans of this sort, and yet in reality she was, helplessly so. She kicked an empty can near her foot. It took a frog hop, clattering into oblivion.

Left alone together in the dim corner, wringing their hands, they chafed silently in discomfort. It was a great relief to both of them when Jailudin finally broke the silence.

"You look wonderful tonight," he said.

"Thanks so much. It's so kind of you to have come. I was afraid you weren't going to show up."

"Are you kidding? I wouldn't miss this for the world," he said and the awkwardness began to dissipate. "Besides, I want to see you again!"

"You're not angry with me, are you?"

"Oh, yes, I'll be angry with you until the next millennium!"

"Maybe people will be more enlightened then!"

"Maybe, but I doubt it. They're too lazy to change."

"You're still angry, I can see."

"I'm not angry, you see. I'm just plain confused. What's keeping you away? I've waited a long, long time for this. Never once in my life have I felt feelings so pure, so unaffectedly genuine. But why do I get a feeling I'm trespassing? Walking into something disallowable. Disallowable! What kind of word is that? Disallowable! Who makes the rules? Who's to say what's allowable or disallowable? It makes real emotions sound like something forbidding. Like abusive language. Something you see on the label of a rap CD. Or on some prescription medicine. Warning, dangerous substance! Children are disallowed to take this!"

"I can see this is getting nowhere," she said, trying hard to maintain her composure. "You don't understand."

"What's to understand? Don't you want to find out how far we can go?" he persisted.

"I don't know how to explain this to you. I just can't stand to see you suffer."

"Can you please stop worrying about me for a moment!"

"You're so full of anger."

"Don't say that. I'm not angry with you!"

"Then, stop this silly barking."

"I'm sorry. I didn't realize I was barking at you."

They fell silent. Why did it always have to come down to this? What was this frustratingly intangible wall that kept pushing them apart? He wanted to leap into the air and revolt against this unyielding blockade that he felt so constricting him, knocking him down over and over into submission. But when he looked at the sublimely smiling face before him, his heart weakened and he acquiesced, like a beaten man, giving up all hope of ever recovering his lost love.

Outside at the gate of the Fair Ground, a flat-bed truck pulled up, hauling a full load of frenetic crowd, wearing red headbands, flailing bamboo spears. As soon as the truck came to a halt, they jumped off, and jostling and scrambling, they charged into the Festival Fair Ground.

There was a great commotion as they fell upon the stands, toppling the goods on display and grappling with the vendors. They ransacked the stalls, grabbing everything on display and then massed toward the main event area.

At first, Sheryl heard plaintive cries from a distance, then as the raffish mob started toward the main stage, she saw the spectators, closed in by the rampaging mass, scattering in fright, screaming and wildly running for their lives. In a brief moment, the frenzied mob tore down the main stage, turning the whole Jakarta Festival Fair Ground into a tumult of maddening chaos.

"It's the looters," Jailudin was suddenly by her side,

pulling her arm away.

MayLin was at his elbow, unable to wrench her eyes from the melee. "What a shame! So much good work put to waste because of this…endless display of stupidity!"

"We have to leave now," Jailudin said, his voice quavering with urgency.

They dashed toward the narrow darkened passage behind the makeshift tent. MayLin came up from the rear, hopping and tottering in her tight Kebaya as crackling flames and blatant shrieks of madness quickly gained upon them.

They emerged on the other end of the Festival Fair Ground. They stood indecisively for a moment in the deserted junction, trying to get an orientation of their exact position when on a sudden a black Mercedes with its headlights doused, swerved out of darkness, pulling up before them.

"Get in, quick!" a familiar voice called out from the driver's seat.

They climbed into the car, which instantly took off, speeding through the Fair Ground, clear out of the compounds bumping hard into the city lights.

Almost instantly, MayLin recognized the man behind the wheel.

"Uncle Tuts!" she exclaimed. "Fancy meeting you here!"

"Don't get wise with me, Missy. You've caused enough problem as it is," he grumbled, not in the least bit enjoying his role as the savior. The little misadventure had apparently caused his heart inconsiderable trauma, for he looked pale and trembling, his sweaty palms gripping on the wheel like his life depended on it.

"You can slow down now, Uncle Tuts!" MayLin said reproachfully.

"We must get as far away as possible. You don't know these people. They're brutal!" he muttered.

"What were you doing there at the Fair Ground, Uncle Tuts?"

"To save your teeny royal behind, that's why!"

"Father sent you, didn't he?"

He kept quiet, eyes fixed on the road, looking once again in the role of the doddering old man being bullied by his beloved child.

"Answer me, Uncle Tuts!"

"I've been watching over you for weeks, Missy!"

"You're keeping an eye on me! He put you to this, didn't he? This is too much!" MayLin exploded. There was a chagrined look on the old man's face as MayLin raged on. He appeared as if he was solely to be blamed for MayLin's tantrums.

Watching from the back seat, Jailudin was greatly amused by how hard the bumbling old man had tried to appease the sulking lady, and how patiently he received her rebuffs. Only the unconditional love of a close kin would allow himself to endure the pesky chiding with such grace. Jailudin envied the old man's privilege. He wished that he had been him, gladly submitting himself to her unreasonable wrath.

The car sped past the city borders, heading toward the outskirts, into the hilly terrain of Sukabumi.

"Now, where are you taking us, Uncle Tuts?"

"Be quiet, Missy," he said. "You'll know soon enough!"

Half an hour later, he suddenly swung the car away from the main thoroughfare, bumping heedlessly onto the unpaved rocky terrain, cutting through the brambles deep into the wilderness.

Finally they came out of the tangling brush into a clearing, at the bottom of the hills with the valleys flickering away miles into the distance. Uncle Tuts let the car cruise slowly to the edge of the rutted path and cut the engine.

"Get out, Missy. He's expecting you," Uncle Tuts said, pointing to the dark green Range Rover, which MayLin immediately recognized to be her father's, parked a few yards away.

12

"*T*his way," it was the unmistakable voice of her father, LeeAng. They picked their way gingerly on the uneven, rugged path toward the rocky ranges where LeeAng stood waving at them. Next to LeeAng in his wind-blown anorak, cigar smoke swirling about him, Jailudin and Sheryl soon discovered, was Uncle Syafudin.

When Jailudin and the group approached the outcropping of rocks, they leaned down, reaching out their hands to help them up. The spectacular view of the hills loomed before them, softly illuminated by the wan moonlight, with myriad of flickering dots streaking unevenly along the terraces, like so many fireflies busy at work.

"This, my dear, is how we should make our contribution," LeeAng said, when MayLin snuggled beside him. "No hues and cries, quietly, under the cover of the night.

Look at them; they could have stayed home with their families, enjoying a peaceful and comfortable life. Instead they chose to come here, leaving everything behind them, their security, their lucrative professions, everything just so that they could make a difference. Now, I call that dedication!"

"What are they doing up there?" Jailudin asked, straining his eye to peer into the hills busily plied by tiny dots of moving dark figures.

"It's our experimental project," Uncle Syafudin answered, puffing at his cigar. "We're trying to help the peasants grow their plants more effectively by providing them with the best quality seeds, fertilizers, pesticides and all available agricultural expertise. Go ahead, take a good look!" He passed the night vision binoculars to Jailudin.

"The men and women you see up there…well, you may not see them so clearly in their disguise…in any case, what you see up there are probably some of the nation's most talented people in the fields of pesticides, irrigation and seeding technology."

Jailudin scanned through the binoculars at the tiny flickers dotting the hills. Amplified through the vision enhancement lens, he could see clearly how, with the help of the dim light from small lanterns, they moved carefully along the terraced terrain, weaving in and out of what appeared to be a chili plantation.

"These are the genuine patriots," LeeAng, in his strident voice, continued. "The brave people of this nation. They've been harassed, scared off and chased after, but they come back undaunted, inspired by nothing less than the spirit of good deeds." Then, almost as if openly reprimanding MayLin, he said sharply. "If we didn't know any better, we would have ventured out there in the open. Recklessly putting people's lives in jeopardy. But you see, we know better than that. The world's not ready for our sincerest gesture of good intentions. They'll look on it with suspicion, like with everything else that we do with heartfelt sincerity. I really can't blame them. They're not used to us being generous or charitable. They're more comfortable to see us greedy, scheming for the big break."

"And the politicians! Beware the mealy-mouthed politicians! They'll always be cunning. They'll always be skewering things. They'll besmirch whatever we try to accomplish, just to stir the pots. Look what happened to your pet project! There's a lot of good that comes out of it!"

"This is what we can do so far," he waved his hand about him, making as if he tried to wrest something out of the intangible midnight air. "Till one day when they're truly ready for us!"

MayLin had never seen her father charged so passionately with emotions. While she was preoccupied with her bold vision to confront the world head on, he had been working behind the scene, quietly plodding along and getting things done. She was filled with great remorse for not having been able to recognize his good intentions any sooner and wasted so much precious time beating on the wrong side of the track.

She held him closely. She had never felt closer to him, or prouder of him. There was not a shadow of doubt now that all along he had stayed true to himself, never once forgetting what truly meant the most to his soul: his conscience.

These thoughts titillated her, invoking in her a newfound spirit. She watched before her a whole new horizon of possibilities. She felt incredible restlessness creeping up on her. She could hardly wait to hurl herself among the volunteers.

"You sly old man!" Jailudin whispered to Uncle Syafudin, who was absorbed in his cigar's smoke. "Why did you keep this from us?"

"All in good time. Things happen for a reason, J! They happen, all in good time. Now, it's your turn; from now on, you must take over. LeeAng and I, we old folks, we're going back to our golf games," he guffawed, visibly delighted that the tiny vision he shared with his golf buddy, LeeAng, had flourished and turned into a full-blown reality. As a result of their work, more farmers would enjoy better results of their toil, and fewer children would go hungry without food. All of this was like a small gift of consolation to him in his old age. A small and almost imperceptible hint of a smile crept up on his face.

"Oh, by the way, J, some people are waiting to see you down there!" He pointed to a solitary, faintly lit tent that sat on the edge of the valley. It looked like some kind of a command post built for the volunteers.

Jailudin, followed by Sheryl and MayLin, picked his way through the treacherous path down into the lush rolling fields of the valley, tickled by whatever it was shrouded in so much mystery. As they approached the tent, two figures came out from behind the mosquito screen door.

They froze, eyes glittering in the moonlight. Then, briskly, one of them pulled away the headgear, shaking loose the glossy raven hair.

"Oh, am I glad to see you!" Sheryl exclaimed, rushing to hug Rosa, who appeared hale and hearty in the stuffy black outfit.

"Sorry to have caused so much trouble to you, J!" Rosa said, in bubbly high spirits. "Excuse us this elaborate disguise, we have to do this to protect ourselves!"

Then, the other figure standing by her side took off the mask. "How are you, J?" It was Randy, Jailudin's man on the street, with the wily beaming smile on his face.

Jailudin and Sheryl could not conceal their astonishment. They grabbed him into their arms, and held him tightly like two excited children welcoming back an old, old friend.

"I knew you'd be up to no good!" Jailudin said. "Man, the things you do! You never stop amazing me. I'm so proud of you, Randy!"

Glancing around, feeling the good vibrations all around him, Randy said with a trace of satisfaction in his voice, "I'm proud of myself, too, J!"

A light rain squalled down from the distance. A churning wall of mists scrolled laterally across the hills. The small group scurried into the tent. They huddled over the warm glow from a paraffin lamp, happy to be reunited at last, and brimming with tales to share with one another.

Meanwhile the volunteers continued undeterred in the light drizzle, working their way through the terrain, terrace by terrace, weaving in and out of the fields, driven by unflagging spirit for their quest.

13

The sound and fury surrounding the fire in the Jakarta Festival Fair Ground remained for weeks the main fodder for rousing political debates and media outcries. There were snapshots of the Great LeeAng, on his way to the Supreme Court for questioning. There were inflamed articles written over the engulfing controversy seriously questioning LeeAng's motives. Some were harshly accusatory, excoriating him for causing reckless public disorder, with a clear intent of inciting the envy from the poor. Rafida, as director of The Center, was also called in. Thanks to Uncle Tuts' men she had emerged unscathed from the fire, but deeply incensed by what had happened. She stood defiantly before the inquiry committee, boldly waggling her finger at them, and in her reedy, shaky voice, condemned each and every one of the committee members for condoning such a heinous crime, making a mockery of the law. She spat before the startled members, calling them shameless cowards who picked on their own people.

Buried underneath the full-blown controversy were snippets of news about miraculous crop results in the outlying areas of Jakarta. A phenomenal growth of a new generation of chili had unexpectedly cropped up on the arid soils of the mountainous regions in Sukabumi. It was bigger, spicier, a stronger variant that was surprisingly more resilient toward the invasion of insects. And in another news item, a group of farmers had found to their surprise sacks of fresh coffee seeds on their doorsteps, with complete, easy-to-follow manuals on how to grow the valuable commodity.

Sheryl loved reading these pieces of amazing news to Jailudin. After reading out each item, she would wonder aloud, "Hmm…wonder who'd do such a thing!" That never failed to elicit a chuckle out of Jailudin.

Other than the scraps of news he got from the tabloids about her and LeeAng's tribulations, he had never seen MayLin again. He had irretrievably lost her to her newfound obsession, roaming the countryside in the dead of night, making miracles happen for peasants. He had lost her to the tightly knit bondage of her family, to the perplexing constrictions of customs that seemed forbiddingly inaccessible to outsiders. He had lost her to a thousand confounding reasons but none of which had anything to do with how they felt about each other.

He mourned this loss, at times perplexed and inconsolably enraged, but over time he began to understand. Maybe she was not running away from him, she was simply incapable of running away from herself. She was held hostage by the history of fear, by the insecurity of standing on her own outside of the warm, protecting enclave. Being invisible, running and disappearing, they all seemed to be part and parcel of her natural instinct honed by years of living precariously.

Maybe he was the one who had to be patient, wait for a decade or two. Wait for the harm to be undone, wait for the barriers to be lowered, the uncomfortable constraints removed, allowing for once whatever that was truthful in human nature to shine through, unimpeded.

Politely but firmly Jailudin turned down Uncle Syafudin's request of carrying on his work with the volunteers. He told the cranky old man, he was never much of a night person, besides he still enjoyed his work in photography. He told him it was his calling; he belonged to the brightly exposed realm of photojournalism. It was what he did best. But not wanting to hurt his feelings, he told Uncle Syafudin he would always make himself available should he ever need his help. Sure enough, it put a smile on the wry old fellow's face.

There was no news about Rizal. Whenever news broke about clashes between the Christians and the Muslims, Jailudin would follow it closely, keeping an eye just in case

Rizal would pop up somewhere in the middle of the fray, waging one of his endless crusades.

Fatima suffered silently. She found in the drowning silence the refuge for her pain. She wallowed herself in this newly discovered quiescent realm where she was sheltered, totally removed from the demands of the outside world. It was a painful sight, but Jailudin knew that nobody could lift her out of the thrall of her own misery, except herself.

Jailudin found himself spending more time in the backyard of his sister's house, shifting the rattan chair around, starting over the ritual of capturing that one elusive image of the ideal house. One day, shocked by what he stumbled upon while peering idly into the gray monstrosity, he rose from the rattan chair. He suddenly saw it: the ideal house looming before his eyes in the grainy monochromatic sharpness of a dream, with plenty of sunlight washing in through the bay windows and the soft satin curtains billowing lackadaisically in the wind. It was so clear in his mind's eye, he felt he could open its door and walk into the living room. The vision haunted him, jostled him out of inertia, galvanizing him like an obsession.

He wakened the whole house, rousing Fatima from her sorrowful slumber, pulling Ronny and his sister away from their computer game, and calling Sheryl. When they all gathered before him in the backyard, he was so excited he became lost for words. They watched him quixotically, seriously thinking that this time he really had gone overboard and become insane.

Wordless and gagging in excitement, he pulled them to the exact spot where he had stumbled upon his vision. There, he pointed at an angle the precise location where some wild growths had begun to take hold on the ground next to what once must have been a window frame but now a junkyard's rubbish scrap amidst a pile of discarded furniture and broken crockery.

"There, over there, it will be the porch," he said, seeing it all so clearly. They lolled their heads, moseying about, quizzically peering into the messy void, and trying to conjure up the image that Jailudin so vividly described.

When finally, hopeless and exhausted by the strain of squinting into emptiness, Sheryl plopped back down on the rattan chair. Cheekily she asked, "What would you call your house, J?"

The question caught him by surprise. It had never occurred to him that he should attach a name to a house, when ordinarily a number would have sufficed. The suggestion, nonetheless, intrigued him and caused him to ponder over it seriously for the rest of the afternoon.

Meanwhile the old contractor, Mr Hariman, was recalled but this time with a new set of layout and instructions. He was told to flatten down the existing structure and rebuild from the scratch on the exact position specified by Jailudin. Glad to have any sort of construction work at all in the deepening recession, he was careful not to display any air of misgiving about Jailudin's request. As they strolled over the site, Jailudin in his rat-a-tat delivery fired away detail after detail. Mr Hariman took everything down on his clipboard, ceaselessly nodding his head.

The house was brought back to life, infused by a wave of fresh energy. Fatima, bloated in her shiftless, grieving silence, was unwittingly drawn into the bustle, slowly awakening to the irresistibly enticing din of life.

Quietly from the side, Jailudin watched how the little project had brought back a semblance of normality to daily routine, as nearly as it was before, except for Rizal's absence.

Jailudin searched among Rizal's old associates from the Octagonal Room, but they seemed wary of his inquiry. They eyed him suspiciously. They had been talks of the disappearances. A number of the regulars from the Octagonal Room had gone missing. Nobody knew of their whereabouts. They were overcome with fear, hearing stories, and all kinds of horror stories, about men being abducted and murdered.

With the house under construction and plenty of assignments to complete at the office, Jailudin was able to purge these asides from his thoughts and focused on work.

Every now and then, he and Sheryl still went out to dinner. But these had become gradually quite rare occasions because Jailudin felt that his sister and the two children needed him in the house.

As if in tacit agreement, they never touched on the subject of that intimate evening. Whenever they had a chance to be together, they deftly shirked the subject, discreetly swept it under the table into murky oblivion. It was somehow conveniently let to fade away, dissolved along with the haze of that evening's alcohol.

But they saw a lot of each other at the office where Sheryl still kept her desk. One day in his office, toward the end of the afternoon, Sheryl sidled over from her corner, and slumped down on the edge of his desk. At first, Jailudin had thought that she was finished with her work and getting ready to go out for her regular round of drinks at the Captain's Bar.

"J, I'm leaving!"

"Wait for me for a few minutes, will you? I just need to finish this…this horrid piece of paperwork," he said. Without Rosa, he had no choice but to do everything himself, including writing the invoices. He had considered hiring a new secretary, but the thought of putting someone on Rosa's seat somehow seemed to him such a flagrant act of transgression, a disservice to Rosa.

"I meant leaving for good, J!"

The words began to get through to him. He looked up, staring at her perplexingly. "But, why, your work here isn't done yet!" In his astonishment, he sounded almost panicky.

"I've got a new assignment. You know how it is. Follow the news where trouble brews."

"Where are you going?"

"Cambodia."

He had once suggested that she should leave for a safer place to continue her work, but now when she approached him by her own will about leaving he felt deeply saddened. But he had expected for some time that something like this would one day take place. He knew it was inevitable. Where she came from, nobody had been able to keep her long enough, and why should it be any different here?

Sheryl belonged to the world. Like the migratory avian creature forever flying in search of clement weather, she had embarked yet again on another journey.

On the day of her departure, he drove her to the airport himself. All through the way to the airport, there were no words exchanged between them. As they fleeted past the peasant houses, rippling evanescent shadows behind groves of palm trees along the toll road, images of the past flipped by before his eyes like an old reel of movies being replayed.

He drove through the Balinese-style redbrick gateway at the entrance and pulled up by the curb where overhead a yellow signboard heralded Terminal D, Departure, and a list of names of airlines. The airport traffic controller, a heavy-set man with his swarthy face glistening with perspiration gave him a signal to get a move on. Jailudin made a gesture that he would be on his way shortly.

He could not get himself out of the driver's seat.

A jumble of sensations crowded into his mind like tumbling water from a broken dam. His hands gripped on the steering wheel, his eyes fixed on the no-stop signpost in front of the car. Sheryl held his arm tenderly for a moment, taking a full, exhaustive look at him, then she turned on the door handle and walked down to the back of the car to hoist down her luggage.

With luggage clattering behind her, she came over to the driver's window.

"I left my address in your drawer. Just in case you get a bit jaded and feel footloose about going on a trip," she cleared her throat, barely able to curb the surge of flooding emotions.

"You'll be back in a week," Jailudin said, suddenly optimistic. "You'll see you'll be back quicker than you know. Something nasty is going to happen and you'll be back. Something terrible, like maybe a bomb take off in Monas Park, or some politician got shot and kaboom, you're back!" His voice trailed off. He faltered and was unable to continue.

"Goodbye, J!" she said and leant over to give him a kiss on his lips. She tugged at the dark blue Samsonite, wobbly clattering along the grimy floor into the departure gate. Everything appeared to him in a shroud of mist. He could not even remember to take one last good look at her and she was gone.

A loud honk jolted him. The traffic controller waddled angrily over, furiously waving him along. He stepped on the gas pedal and the car lurched forward and, as if propelled by a will of its own, ambled aimlessly back toward the city.

Half way out of the airport, his cellular phone buzzed. He flipped open the handset and right away recognized Sheryl's voice.

"I'd meant to ask you what name you've come up with for the house," she asked, her husky voice drowned by the clamoring din in the background.

For a moment, Jailudin deluded himself into thinking that she had not gone away after all. She was just a block away and at any moment she would turn up and all was well again. They would maybe go to have a drink at the Captain's Bar.

He smiled, then unexpectedly it blurted out of his mouth, "PlayGround!" He repeated it to himself several times, and then said, nodding his head approvingly, "Yes, that's what I'll call it!"

She laughed, "I like it! It's so right." Then, there was a click and the line went dead.

All through the way back to his sister's, he rolled the syllables on his tongue, playing with them to hear how they sounded to his ears. The more often he heard himself say them aloud, the more he liked them. And as if the missing piece of the jigsaw puzzle finally put in place, he peeled through the veil of grainy monochromatic image and for the first time saw his house clearly, awash in full resplendence of its true colors: bright and loudly colorful.

He drew a deep breath. Faintly he could smell a hint of frangipani in the air.